the **americas**

The Last Reader

David Toscana

Translated by Asa Zatz

Texas Tech University Press

This book is typeset in Monotype Fairfield. The paper used in this book meets the minimum requirements of ANSI/NISO Z39.48-1992 (R1997). ∞

Designed by Barbara Werden

Library of Congress Cataloging-in-Publication Data
Toscana, David, 1961–
[Último lector. English]
        The last reader / David Toscana ; translated by Asa Zatz.
                p. cm. — (The Americas)
        Summary: "A small town in the Mexican desert has a library where few are interested in books. The only reader is the librarian who sees everything through the lens of literature. When a girl is found dead in the librarian's well, he uses novels to lead police directly to the murderer"
—Provided by publisher.
        ISBN 978-0-89672-664-2 (hardcover: alk. paper)
        I. Zatz, Asa. II. Title.

PQ7298.3.O78U4813 2009
863'.64—dc22   2009024343

Printed in the United States of America
09 10 11 12 13 14 15 16 17 / 9 8 7 6 5 4 3 2 1

Texas Tech University Press | Box 41037 | Lubbock, Texas 79409-1037 USA
800.832.4042 | ttup@ttu.edu | www.ttup.ttu.edu

The Last Reader

The bucket slips down the well until it strikes a surface firmer than water making a sound Remigio has already been expecting. It hasn't rained in almost a year, and since July the people have been coming together every afternoon at the Archangel Gabriel chapel to pray. But September is here and not a drop of anything, even spit, from the sky. Now and then there will be dew on the leaves and windowpanes at daybreak, but hardly long enough for even the early risers to notice, since the sun dries up all the moisture in Icamole as soon as it appears over the village.

Rain clouds approached once from the east, and the people clambered up the nearest hills to urge them on. Here we are, come on, we're thirsty, and some women opened umbrellas to make a show of their unshakable faith, a faith insufficient for moving mountains, not Friar's Hill, in any case, twenty kilometers away, while all looked on in disappointment at the way the clouds bumped against its peaks and slopes and emptied their precious load right there. Neither the first nor the last time that Friar's Hill had robbed them of hope, which is why neighboring Villa de García remained green while in Icamole the ditches are raceways for opossums. Remigio pulls on the rope and lets the bucket down again. It makes the same sound: a thump. He would have found harp music or a siren song coming up from below just as disagreeable; the only voice of his well had to be a splash.

He checks the rope and is now sure that there is trouble. He knows the well is eight meters deep and that the rope is knotted at exactly that point. According to his reckoning there has to be at least half a meter of water there, more than enough for the avocado tree and for him to wash that morning and other mornings, to be followed by a turn in Icamole, hair tousled by the wind, face cool, teeth clean, saying good morning to the women with stiff hair bound up in a kerchief and the men with dusty faces and dirty fingernails in that village of Icamole without moisture other than sweat and the drums of water brought in on Melquisedec's wagon from Villa de García. With the drought came poverty and the day when the soda man said It doesn't pay me to deliver all this way to sell this few bottles. Melquisedec's water is free: he siphons it out of a communal reservoir in Villa de García, and the state pays for him and his mules, which pull the wagon on the easy trip there and the heavy haul back.

To prevent waste, the people say Melquisedec's water is for drinking, not washing feet, which is what prompts Remigio to provoke them with his freshly washed face. I drink, his expression tells them, I shower, and I even sprinkle my avocado tree with no need for the water wagon, although, when asked, his unhesitating reply is that his well is just as dry as the rest. He swings the rope back and forth several times, without feeling the bucket nip at the half meter of water, and comes to the conclusion that an obstacle of some kind is in the way. This wouldn't be the first thirsty animal to give him trouble. Three years before, he had to pull out a coyote, which, to make matters worse, put up a defense as though Remigio were an enemy and not its rescuer. Nonetheless, he didn't hold it against the creature. He knows that any death is preferable to dying of thirst. He goes for a kerosene lamp, which he ties to the rope and lets down into the earth's dark gullet. The first thing he makes out is the glint of two wide-open eyes, then the pale, girlish face like in an old photograph, and, finally, long, black hair, still neatly combed. He figures that her face has been struck by the bucket a dozen times and, after staring at it for a couple of minutes, comes to the conclusion that she is not blinking.

When he was ten years old, Remigio considered wells a place for doing mischief, such as spitting in them, dropping in goat shit, one or two little balls at a time, and even pissing once into Señora Cleotilde's. All the same, he considered it out of line when one of his friends threw a dead rat into Melquisedec's well. Fun lay not in the damage done but in the doing of it on the sly, and this evaporated when Remigio found out that all the wells were connected and that piss which went into Señora Cleotilde's, even though diluted, would end up in all the other houses. Remigio believes that the low point of this underground network of canals is on his property; otherwise, how to explain why his well should still have water when all the rest have run dry? Pissing or throwing in a rat could pass, but not a girl. He dismisses the idea that she might have fallen in accidentally; in that case he would be looking at panties, not a face.

He runs to the house for his machete and then into the orchard, brandishing the weapon and banging it against dry branches in the event that whoever brought the girl might still be lurking about. He also looks outside for anybody who might be spying from up in a tree behind adobe walls. He then stands still, almost without breathing, in an effort to catch the slightest sound and is able to make out several, but at a distance: a woman complaining that her foot hurts, a man clearing his throat, a child in tears yelling Paco hit me; the unmistakable voice of Fatso Antúnez threatening to punch Paco in the nose. Remigio drops the machete and returns to the well. He moves the kerosene lamp close to the face and waits until the swaying stops, for the shifting shadows give a sensation of the body moving. The girl is lying on her back, a good part of her torso out of the water, looking almost comfortable. He gathers a handful of pebbles and drops them in one by one. The first three miss the mark. The fourth bounces off her forehead or nose, Remigio thus verifying that the face is showing no reaction. It seemed to him from the very beginning that she was absolutely dead, but, at the same time, the age-old dream of rescuing a girl is not so easily relinquished.

He fetches another rope with a rusty hook at one end, which he lowers, dangling it over the body until it snags somewhere; he would prefer that place to be an armpit, because he doesn't like the idea of hauling the girl out like a fish. He listens intently as he pulls on the rope. Although he no longer expects to hear a moan, it is best to make sure. After being lifted only a few centimeters, she makes the splattering sound Remigio wanted to hear from the bucket. Now, as he imagines lacerated flesh and bloodstained water, no matter how clean the girl might have been, even the thought of brushing his teeth with that water gives him a queasy feeling. He realizes that the hook is probably not a good idea regardless of where it might catch, armpit, mouth, nostril, or crotch, and opts for lassoing her. As he fashions a loop, he keeps repeating lasso, lasso aloud, because his mind insists on calling it a noose. Again he lowers the rope, rotating it and letting it swing until it takes hold somewhere. He pulls on it carefully, and when it seems certain that the lasso has tightened, he begins raising the body rapidly. It comes up suspended by the left wrist. Had it caught around the neck he would have raised her just as well, but by the wrist couldn't be better.

He grasps her hand as soon as he sees her come into view and is surprised that he has no feeling of revulsion. Once before he had to lift a dead body and almost threw up. But you are different, he says to the girl, you should have seen the other guy, old and fat, besides being swollen and naked because he drowned in a pool. He stretches her out on the ground and pulls down the eyelids. The left one obeys; the right one folds slowly back leaving the eye wide open. White socks, flowered dress, and one patent-leather shoe. Her face appears very smooth, with no signs of violence or marks from the bucket; only a bit of dirt on the left cheek he tries to remove until he suddenly realizes it is a birthmark. In her right sleeve there is a tear made no doubt by the ineffective hook.

Remigio has never been sociable, nor is he given to taking notice of schoolgirls, but he is certain about never having seen this one before, which means she is not from Icamole. A girl like this would have taken part in some performance or other, might have recited at a church affair, and even if she sounded awful, everybody would have applauded her roundly. However, I am also sure, he says to himself, now looking around him again, a girl like this is never going to be given up for lost.

They passed the time on the ten-mile trek talking about women and gulping short slugs from a bottle of bourbon shunted back and forth between them. Tom laughed at all Murdoch's stories no matter whether he was being serious or funny. He told one about a prostitute he had known in Mexico, and Tom laughed at every sentence, particularly when Murdoch was explaining the kind of problems that can come up in living with a woman who doesn't understand your language. Right after that he briefly mentioned a blonde he had loved, and Tom laughed again. Behind them a black man, walking, his hands tied and a rope around his neck, exhausted, forced to quicken his stride whenever Tom's and Murdoch's horses lengthened theirs. Here we are, said Tom, stopping at the halfway point on the bridge over the Colorado River. With the beams creaking under the weight of the horses and holes in some of the boards a foot could go through, it gave the impression of not being a very sturdy structure. Leaning over the railing, Murdoch watched the reflection of the moon in the rushing waters now under their feet but soon on the way to another county, another state, with a swiftness that perhaps they themselves would never enjoy. He spat into space and turned around to his horse, pulling the noose tighter around the unfortunate prisoner's neck. Any idea what you're in for now, you scum out of hell? The Negro shook his head, though it was evident from his terrified expression that he knew. Both of them hauled him to the railing, where they forced him to look down, his eyes bulging with horror, at the water Murdoch had just regarded with pleasure. The black man no longer struggled. He preferred getting it over with to the humiliation of being dragged along like a dog, dodging horse turds and listening to the blather of drunks. Got something you want to say before you cash in? Murdoch asked. The black man nodded and, trying to keep his voice from trembling, declared, There is a God who doesn't differentiate between skin colors, who loves blacks and whites alike . . .

Lucio snorts and bangs the book shut. Two hundred pages to get to the point of listening to this Negro preaching like a Sister of Mercy. What a fraud. The back cover claims that the reader will be plunged into the very depths of the human soul, that there are places in which hell itself resides in skin color, in which the forces of good and evil clash with portentous consequences. The only thing now lacking, Lucio says to himself, is a definition of good and evil, because Tom and Murdoch would have done the world a big favor if they had heaved the Negro overboard before letting him speak. There are a hundred or so pages to go, but he has no intention of continuing his reading. He looks at the cover: *The Color of Heaven*, by Brian MacAllister. He imagines the author to have been a white blowhard who sang in a Protestant church as a boy; surely he doesn't have the courage to allow the Negro to die right after mentioning God? Will the sheriff arrive? Other Negroes? An angel? Will the Negro be able untie himself and kill his enemies? It no longer makes any difference. Besides, a translator who doesn't convert miles into kilometers is not to be trusted, and I have no idea what MacAllister may have written, but I am sure it must have been something very different from scum out of hell. He takes a rubber stamp from his desk drawer and stamps the cover: WITHDRAWN. Getting up slowly, allowing back and waist to adjust to the new position, he goes to stand outside his door. A woman passing by is carrying half a kilo of tortillas, which cause Lucio's mouth to water. She smiles at him in a wordless greeting, to which he replies by telling her that MacAllister is an incompetent hack and continues talking to himself in a whisper. Imagine: he mentions the expression of horror on the Negro's face but doesn't pursue it in depth; he should have told me how his thick red lips, crisscrossed with threads of spittle, were trembling or at least how the moon shone on the whites of his eyes. Using the word *horror* is a deception on the part of a writer seeking to create a nonexistent tension, because it is obvious that the Negro is not going to die. Everything is so obvious: the whites talking about a prostitute and the black man invoking God, the whites swilling bourbon and the black's sweat not even stinking. Lucio goes back to his desk and opens the book to the last page in order to confirm the anticipated moral. The old woman had been rocking little Jimmy for hours. With the approaching dawn, her snow-white hair seemed to glow with an inner light. Grandma, why do such things have to happen? She raised her eyes; the sun was painting a yellow stripe across the horizon. When you grow up you will understand, she answered. Just remember that it is the color of the soul not of the skin that really makes people different. Jimmy smiled and closed his eyes. In the distance, the Carmichaels' cock crowed, letting the world know that life goes on, and always will. Lucio shakes his head and goes out again. He gets halfway down the street, where he waits for two fat women, who stop talking when they see him. Would you care to read a book? Go on in, it's free. You might enjoy *The Creative Temptation*. It's about a seminarian with a passion for painting, especially nudes. Cut it out, Lucio, you're too old now for that stuff, one of them says. Instead of wasting your time reading, come and pray with us for the drought to end. Lucio feels his temples beginning to throb as the women move on, swaying their hips; one is carrying a dead chicken; the other, a parasol. This much is certain: the seminarian wouldn't want to paint nudes of those women. He loved art but what he loved most was having young women with nothing on in front of him. Will I find salvation? Larissa asked him after her dress came off. The seminarian handed her a bunch of lilies, directed her to raise her right arm, taking care not to cover her breasts with them, and turned back to his easel. Of course you will find salvation, he replied, because now you are no longer Larissa but Saint Agnes at the door of a brothel, and you will soon be adorning Brother Esteban's room, and Brother Esteban will pray for you every night so that he may be accorded the grace of touching your body before he dies.

Although the dead chicken does not look tempting to him, Lucio pictures it plucked, cooked, and in the center of a table. A drumstick, he whispers, and imagines dipping it into a bowl of mashed beans. Sex can be satisfied with the imagination, he says to himself, but hunger is only made worse. He goes into the library and locks the door. He feels humiliated at having suggested that those women ought to read; he must stifle the temptation to follow them and ask for something to eat, he must be strong as Brother Esteban was not. If just one of those Icamole women were to become interested in reading, things would be different. I came to see what book you would recommend, Don Lucio and, incidentally, to bring you some tacos; or, My mother sent for a novel and asked me to drop this soup off for you. That's the way the priests have it. That's how it should be with me.

Opening a book, he begins to read. He has made sure that the novel is a recent one, for those don't bother to describe details of a meal unless they are by women writers, or the author is a Latin American who, at the outset of his career, believed that writing cured social ills and, as time went on, preferred to cater to the ladies in patent leather who asked, flattery and coquetry added, for his autograph, and the allure of things foreign, for once upon a time I was of the people, my dear ladies, but now I am Frenchified or Germanized or Bulgarianized. My character, who used to wield a dagger, now raises a glass of wine; he himself once bunked in an alley and now complains when his hotel room doesn't have an ocean view. He had discarded just one such novel only the day before. The narrator seated at the table was saying, Sara chose a splendid bottle of Château Certan-Marzelle '98 to go with the Perigourdin salad, *cocotte de porc à l'ananas*, a Coulommiers brie, and instead of a dessert, *crêpes aux moules* prepared with an exquisite *vin de paille*. Those lines and the description of other dishes and bottles and terms that ran on in italics stimulated not the slightest reaction in his stomach. With those foreign names it's all the same to me whether they are talking about food or car parts; those bottles could be bottles of oil, and maybe *cocotte* was some kind of gear. He withdrew the novel at page 39. He was familiar with other books by Antonio Pedraza from the days when his publications, not his world travels, were listed in his biography; in those days his prose did express something, was concerned with people who don't own calling cards and walk along streets called street, not *rue*. This fellow no longer writes for me, Lucio said. He stood up and let the novel drop. Antonio Pedraza, rest in peace.

And resentment against that novelist assuaged his hunger, which was not to resurge until the sight of the tortillas and the chicken.

The town without water and I without food. Not bad for the ending of a novel, he says to himself. The people leave Icamole and I starve to death.

The goat bell can be heard all over Icamole, which is not to say much: forty houses, more or less, in a ragged line like badly parked vans along a crossing of unpaved streets; a few, like Remigio's, surrounded by adobe walls; others, by a mesh or barbed-wire fence to keep goats and chickens from getting out and predatory animals in particular from getting in; others, protected by natural walls of prickly pear cactuses planted in a line very close to one another; and, finally, a few more that have nothing to hide or protect seem like rocks out in an open field. The women and some men leave their chores to pick up bottles, pitchers, jugs and go toward where Melquisedec is clanging his bell. They form five lines, one behind each drum, and all in turn fill their receptacles without pushing or complaining, for they know that there is water enough for everybody; they are surprised only at seeing Remigio there with a plastic container. Señora Vargas approaches him and, even though she is standing close to his ear, addresses him in a loud voice. People say you are still getting water from your well. No, Señora, Remigio answers, the thing is, I live alone, so everything stretches further for me. He doesn't explain to her that he still has water enough for bathing, as well as for the avocado tree, and only for that, since the law of survival of the fittest specifies that you should never drink water where a dead animal has been floating, and the girl, in this case, is nothing but a dead animal with body fluids that will not arrive diluted at all the houses but will remain in his well, thick and fragrant in his half-meter pool. I rather thought, Señor Treviño says, that you would have cases of beer. Hoping that his clean face is being noticed, Remigio replies, I do, but I have just two bottles and am saving them for a special occasion. The words are hardly out of his mouth before he is suffused with a feeling of pity for everyone: there being no social classes, differences in Icamole are evident in small things like a clean face, hands without calluses, the pursed lips of that woman, Señora Urdaneta, now drinking her ration and saying that her pitcher is made of finest-quality clay. My son-in-law brought it from Tlaquepaque and it is hand-painted; just look, these are sunflowers and they even seem real. Remigio examines the pitcher as though he would like to smash it to smithereens. He has no doubt that the girl's dress would be the envy of all those women.

Melquisedec oversees from his seat on the wagon, gesticulating his displeasure every time somebody spills a few drops of water. A waste of my mules' efforts, he complains, with nobody paying attention. After all receptacles have been filled, he will empty the remaining water into troughs for the goats and his own mules.

I have an announcement for you, Melquisedec raises his voice when a fair number of people are gathered around his wagon. A little girl is missing over in Villa de García. She is the daughter of a widow woman from Monterrey, and the two of them were on a visit to these parts. The authorities are asking us to be on the lookout for anything out of the ordinary, especially if we spy a stranger. In that case, they request that we hold him and let them know. After a few moments of silence broken only by the gurgling of water, Señor Hernández asks, You mean, if we notice a stranger we should grab him? What if he puts up a fight? Do we give him a beating and tie him up? In whose house are we supposed to hold him? Melquisedec shrugs. What does the girl look like? Señora Vargas asks. I have no idea, Melquisedec answers. How old is she? His shoulders remain shrugged. I don't know that either, but I promise to have further information for you tomorrow.

Remigio kisses the edge of his container and takes a long drink from it. What a difference in taste between fresh water and stagnant.

Lucio looks up from *Autumn in Madrid* as the door opens. Without removing his forefinger from the last word read in the middle of page 63 he asks, What brings you here? Remigio closes the door, goes to the desk, and deposits a paper bag close to the book. Avocados, he says, and tortillas. Lucio inserts a bookmark. And what would I be wanting with avocados? Remigio takes them out of the bag: there are two, the smooth skins so black they look purple. The aroma of the tortillas pervades the atmosphere just the way that woman's did in the morning. It's no secret that you're starving. Fix yourself a few tacos, there's a knife in the bag. So as not to appear overanxious, Lucio opens *Autumn in Madrid* again and runs his eyes briefly over the next few sentences. Natalia, my Natalia, I have mentioned to you a hundred and one times that the city is a shop window that displays my sadnesses, my need for you, my inability to appreciate beauty that does not emanate from your countenance. Mentioning it once would be enough for me, says Lucio, reaching into his desk drawer for the WITHDRAWN stamp. Another one of those oily Spaniards with more guile than style, he mutters, but at least it rains in Madrid, and the girls wear short skirts. He slices the first avocado into four pieces and places each on a tortilla. He knows he is hungry enough to eat everything at once but decides to put the other avocado away. To open conversation, Remigio says, I didn't see you getting water from Melquisedec. Yesterday I filled my jug and it's hardly even half empty. Then you wouldn't have heard the news. Lucio shakes his head as he bites into his taco. Eating now, he wonders what would have become of him if Remigio hadn't come around. Reading makes time pass for me, and I can forget about being hungry, but at night it's impossible to sleep. *Autumn in Madrid* opens in a restaurant with two waiters unhooking a couple of hams from over the counter with which they pummel one another as an African immigrant outside looks on from the sidewalk. It is fun for the waiters; for Lucio it means condemnation to a sleepless night thinking of pork. In any case, this opening caught his attention. The two hams are from one animal and after each blow dealt by the waiters, the author goes back to the slaughterhouse to describe the arrival of the hog in a stinking truck and the preparations for its butchering. At last one of those Spaniards who know how to write, he said to himself. But reading on, it turns out that, just as the slaughterer is sharpening his knife, the scene cuts before the death of the hog to fix on a table next to a window where a young man sits watching the ladies of Madrid go by as he composes a love letter, which by the time Remigio entered, had stretched over to page 63. I don't know why I am confessing all this to you, the young man writes to his sweetheart, and neither does Lucio have the remotest idea. Rather, he imagined a slaughterhouse novel: raw in its killing of hogs, light in the earthiness of waiters who serve the meat of those animals, and subtle in its implications, with the presence of the African immigrant passing by. Remigio clenches his fists before speaking: Melquisedec said that a girl is missing in Villa de García. Lucio picks up the book and goes to the heavy door leading to the adjoining room. Although closed with a lock and rusty latch, the door has an opening in the upper part covered by a short curtain. He calls the author, Jordi Ventura, a dirty name. Too many pages just to be telling me that the young man is sad because his sweetheart has left him. I lost my wife, a marvelous woman, not one of those Madrid chippies, and I'd be satisfied to find half a page about her. He pulls the curtain aside and tosses *Autumn in Madrid* through the opening. Forgive him not, oh Lord, he says, for he knew what he was doing. He returns to his desk and addresses the remaining tacos. Today was not a good one for me with my books. I have already withdrawn two. He finishes eating and gives his teeth a going-over with the nail of his little finger. Remigio raps on the desk in a show of impatience. Are you going to pay attention to me or not? Lucio smiles. I have listened to every word and observed your gestures and movements to the point where I am willing to bet that you didn't bring me avocados because I am hungry; in fact, I am beginning to think they have something to do with the missing girl. She is not missing, Remigio explains, not for me, at least; I found her dead in my well and don't know what do with her. Of course, Lucio says, I should have figured as much because avocados have a certain resemblance to eggplants, and Zimbrowski brings eggplants to his father when he confesses to having murdered Enzia, the telegrapher's daughter. Zimbrowski bursts out crying and kneels down, begging pardon. I didn't want to do it, it was the alcohol, the urge, the craziness; it wasn't me, because I was somebody else that night, a monster, a contemptible being and not your son. His father cuffs him, calls him a coward, throws the eggplants out of the window, and turns him over to the police himself. When the telegrapher learns the truth about his daughter's death, he composes a cable in Morse code: Zimbrowski, may you be a thousand times damned; and transmits it to all offices. You didn't throw the avocados out the window, Remigio says. A silence prevails during which Lucio puts the knife back in the bag. There are other differences, he says. Zimbrowski's father loved Enzia; he considered her his granddaughter and always lived his life in accordance with a military code of honor. The dishonor of hell before the hell of dishonor, he always said. I did not kill her, Remigio raises his voice in an effort to close out the Zimbrowski story and begin his own. In few words he relates his finding of the dead girl and the problems in getting her out of the well, closing her eyes, and setting her out to dry. To dry? interrupts Lucio. Your well has water? I have her in the house, on the floor, on a towel in the kitchen. Lucio looks at the paper bag and realizes that there is an abyss between avocados and eggplants. Who told you I am going hungry? I have a dead girl. I believe that should be our topic of conversation. Lucio remains indifferent and goes to a pile of sealed and banded cartons. I still have a lot of reading to do; it is going to take me years to classify all these books. Remigio, sullen, goes over to him. It's no secret to anybody that you lost your job long ago. They say your money is all gone, that you don't go to Romelia's store anymore, that you're getting thin and looking sick. There's nothing dishonorable about a son helping his father. Lucio sits down again; he settles back and closes his eyes. What do you know about this girl? Only that she's the daughter of a widow who was visiting in Villa de García; they are searching for her and asked Icamole folks to be on the lookout. Lucio shakes his head, then he speaks slowly in a low voice, almost as though he were entering a dream state. You had her in your hands, in your well, you pulled her out, you brought her into the kitchen. No doubt you've been looking at her and very likely other things; I suspect that you are still not telling me everything. I did not kill her, Remigio insists. Of that

I am sure. Lucio opens his eyes, his expression unconcerned: It was the alcohol, the urge, the craziness. Remigio pulls a chair over in front of the desk and sits. He has trouble getting the words out. She must be thirteen years old, her skin is very white and her hair is very black like avocado peel; she has on a party dress and is missing a shoe. Is that all? Yes, that's all. How did she die? Remigio keeps quiet. Were her clothes in order? Are her panties in place? Yes. Yes. Coming out of his lethargy, Lucio straightens up. Did you check them carefully? The criminal sometimes makes a mistake and puts them back on with the label on the belly button. I'm not interested in what happened. Remigio goes to the water jug and takes a few swallows. All I want is to keep anything from happening to me. You'd better be interested; your fate won't be the same if the panties are on the other way around; that's what got Zimbrowski hanged. I think I made a mistake coming to you. Hesitating a moment about taking back the remaining avocado, Remigio goes to the door. Wait. Lucio raises his voice: If the girl is overweight and has curly hair, you don't have to worry, the truth will soon come out; her mathematics teacher pushed her down the stairs in a fit of temper because the dunce didn't even know the sixes table; but he himself is going to confess and explain where he threw the body, so the best thing for you to do is to go back and throw her down the well. Neither fat nor curly-headed, Remigio says, the one in my house is terrific. Bad luck, says Lucio, then, yes, you are in trouble, because the girl has to have light-colored eyes and a birthmark on her left cheek, and there will be no mathematics teacher to take the blame. Remigio moves closer; he does not recall having told him that. Light-colored eyes, yes, one open and the other closed, and a birthmark on the left side. Lucio slaps his thighs with both hands. He smiles with satisfaction at having connected on his second try. Then her name is Babette, he says. She was twelve years old, and I will describe her to you as only Pierre Laffitte could. He hurries to the bookcase and takes down a volume. After turning pages for a few moments he begins to read. At twelve years of age, Babette was as vain as an older woman and liked to wear dresses tight-fitting around the waist that showed a bit of calf. She loved windy days, because the tousling of her intensely black hair caused her sad, light-gray eyes to sparkle, eyes that were always fixed, beyond the contours of her dainty nose, upon the horizon. Though her skin was very white, so much so that the blue veins showed through on her arms and cheeks, she did not give the impression of being sickly. Quite the contrary; if one were to study her closely, he would find her firmly fleshed, sturdy for her age and almost masculine were it not for her budding forms, which presaged a shape of the kind that causes voices to fall silent when she is going by. On moonlit nights, her pallor made her appear as though touched by the divine. Radiance would be the quality that best defined her, her eyes, hair, countenance, skin, and even her shoes always shined. Radiance, particularly in her smile, the few times she smiled. But destiny never bestows favors without exacting a return, and everything in Babette that was grace and charm was to result in her perdition. Perhaps the birthmark on her left cheek was a hardened tear that served as a harbinger of what was to come.

Lucio takes turns around his desk as he reads. Remigio had begun listening with arms folded, fed up, his interest piqued, however, as the words sink in that cannot but be comparable to the description of the girl in his house. In novels, girls were made to be desired, abused, or murdered; in addition to *The Death of Babette*, Lucio points to various places in one bookcase. We have *Pink Stockings*, *City without Children*, *The Orphanage of the Innocents*,

The Telegrapher's Daughter, and many others. Of course, I am speaking of novels written by men; women writers let the girls grow up and cause them heartbreak. And what happens to Babette? It is getting dark. Lucio goes to the door and, after checking that the street is empty, comes back in. It all takes place in Paris, July 14, 1789. I am not going to explain to you why that is an important date, but there was a mob out on the streets spoiling for violence. Babette finds herself caught by surprise in the midst of the throng and begins to run because those people are not of her class. When they see her in such a fine dress, the party dress you told me about, some of them chase her. They carry sticks and mattocks and actual weapons. Babette, in tears, runs into an entranceway and out of desperation rings the bell. The door opens, closes just in time, and Babette is never seen again. Then what? Remigio is disappointed; this story is telling him nothing. Hearing it is not the same as reading it; there happens to be symbolism between the bell rung by Babette, that of her perdition, and the ones sounded by the Parisians, those of their freedom. The author was undoubtedly a monarchist. He intended to give the impression . . . But, Remigio interrupts, what happens to Babette? The novel ends there. The last sentence says . . . Lucio opens the book at the back cover and consults the table of contents before reading. Little bells, shouting, and big bells; shouting inside and shouting outside and more bells, poor Babette, poor thing, bells and more bells, a country that believes it is free, a girl who has no beliefs.

A story can't end like that, Remigio protests. Of course it can, and there is no doubt about the ending. Pierre Laffitte has already said it in the title and so avoids repeating it in the plot. What matters is that you and I already know a little more than the rest of the readers; we now know that Babette ended up in a well. But where am I going to end up? Do your books say? I was reading one today: two men on horseback are leading another man on foot, hands tied, dragged along by a rope around his neck. I can imagine you in that trek from here to Villa de García; you will be saying, I did not kill her, and somebody will call you a coward and cuff you, because there aren't any bridges or rivers on that route. Although I can see you just as well digging a grave that swallows Babette forever like a door that shuts. I also have thought about burying her, but with the ground so dry, it's hard to disguise a hole because, no matter how much you tamp it down, the scar remains. My other option is to wait for midnight, take her far away and throw her somewhere behind a hill to the coyotes. But in this town there's always somebody with his eyes peeled, particularly now that I feel that I'm being watched by whoever threw the girl in my well. He must be waiting for me to make a mistake to raise a hue and cry, and if not today, some other day, but that person will end up blowing the whistle. I advise you, Lucio begins, but Remigio interrupts him. I didn't come for advice; all I wanted was to tell you about the girl because, if things begin to get out of hand, I would like for you to be my ally and explain to everybody that this girl appeared in my well without my having anything to do with it. Lucio nods slowly and goes to open the door. He imagines that the only way of doing what Remigio asks is to take the blame himself. Son, whether you do the right thing or the wrong thing, you can count on me, he tells him, quickly regretting how shallow his words sound, worthy of a black man about to be thrown into the Colorado River.

Lucio contemplates the façade of his *biblioteca* in the snippet of moonlight. Part of the plaster has fallen off; for that reason only the word *Bibliote* is legible; the last two letters had appeared as crumbs on the ground after an ordinary night, with no special force other than age and neglect having brought them down, letters he himself had written unevenly with pitch on the day the first shipment of books arrived: 507 volumes, of which only 130 were to appear on the shelves. The rest bore the WITHDRAWN stamp.

In that batch, he was particularly surprised by the novel *Fishes of the Land*, by Klaus Haslinger, the renowned German naturalist who became a writer. Unintrigued by the plot, which concerned Fritz and Petra, a couple who visit various areas in search of a place to settle, it seemed to Lucio a mere device on Haslinger's part to enable him to talk about land, plants, and animals using both ordinary and technical names, and some in Latin. However, just as he was about to discontinue reading, the couple arrived at a place which Lucio had no doubt was Icamole. Fritz felt such a rush of enthusiasm that he took hold of Petra's hand and squeezed it. You're hurting me, she said. He answered, Look, Petra, our Eden. As soon as they started down into the little valley, they felt themselves in another world: the dirt road had turned into one of reddish sand that crunched under every step; all they had to do was bend over to see snails, seashells, fossil trilobites, and nautiluses lying close to the surface. The vegetation, too, was strange: slender plants growing there with dozens of shoots that sought the sky and danced to the rhythm set them by the wind, like seaweed swaying with the current, eager to caress the surface. Rocks scattered about the entire terrain lay in a pattern only the waters could have been responsible for, since they seemed not buried but set into place. Fritz pointed out the two hills in front of them, one steep, the other with a slight slope, both with a cleft at the same height. That is where the waves would be striking, he said, pointing to the cleft. Both were familiar with the earth's Precambrian past under the waters, but this place made them feel like the sea had disappeared no more than a matter of moments before. Petra imagined that if she sharpened her gaze she would be able to make out fish beating their fins desperately, unable to breathe, but she did not wish to convey her idea because the fish she had in mind were *Barbus barbus*, a freshwater species, as everybody knows. They continued on their way downhill toward the hamlet below. The search is over, said Fritz; this is where we will settle. Yes, Petra agreed, we shall dwell at the bottom of the sea. And as they approached, Fritz remarked that if the village were not so modest in appearance it could be taken for Atlantis.

For Lucio, comparing Icamole with Atlantis seemed nonsensical, a foolishness on Fritz's or Haslinger's part, and he didn't know about *Barbus barbus*, but went on reading anyway. The story of Fritz and Petra ended badly: they were never able to adapt to local customs; accordingly, the inhabitants, outraged because they regarded the newcomers with a different language as a threat, as a pair of intruders more concerned with teaching than learning, decided to expel them. When the pair left the valley as they had entered, hand in hand, somebody threw a stone that struck Fritz in the head. Although the wound bled, it was not serious. He bent down to pick up the stone and noted that it bore the impression of a fossil trilobite. He put it in his pocket, but, on second thought, threw it back on the ground. He wanted no tangible proof of their stay in that place, preferring the always more pleasant memory. He continued walking and said, If we cannot be fish, we will have to be reptiles. Lucio did not, nor cared to, understand the ending; all that interested him was the paragraph that described the couple's arrival in Icamole.

Nobody else shared his interest. No German ever came here, they said to him; it is indeed a place that looks like Icamole, but Icamole it is not and never will be. And Lucio's insistence turned against him, since by the time opening day of the library came, the people were full of arguments against books: books are concerned with things that don't exist, they are lies. If I put my hands near the fire, one man said, I get burned; if I stick myself with a knife, I bleed; if I drink tequila, I get drunk; but a book does nothing to me unless you throw it in my face. Others laughed at this sally, and the matter was considered settled. Nevertheless, Lucio decided to name the library in honor of Klaus Haslinger and inscribed his name with pitch on one side of the door in the same kind of uneven letters.

Time passed and Lucio had no cause for complaint: the paymaster came every two weeks, and from time to time a package of books arrived in Villa García for him. Besides, he could spend the day reading with very few interruptions. However, a new state government came in, which very soon made its presence felt. First, it ordered that the library be given the name of a teacher, Fidencio Arriaga, a leader of his union, who was knifed in a fracas, and

Lucio was sent a metal plaque with which to cover the name of Haslinger. Subsequently, for reasons of enhanced utilization of funding, all librarians were required to submit a quarterly report listing the number of visitors, books loaned, books lost, as well as consultations of encyclopedias and school texts. Lucio had no need for records to fill out the report: attendance at the outset averaged three visitors a week, all students at the Icamole school and in every case for the purpose of consulting the encyclopedia. After he decided to give the encyclopedia to the school, it became an illusory event for anybody to come in for a book.

After his third report, Lucio was officially notified that the Fidencio Arriaga Library was closed for an indefinite period, for which reason it would no longer receive books or financial support as of that moment. Lucio responded with an irate letter to the state authorities asserting that, just as water is most needed in the desert and medicine in sickness, so books are indispensable where nobody reads. Furthermore, he declared, the library is installed on my property and nobody has a right to compel me to close the doors of my house. He received no answer. Nor did the paymaster visit him again.

The first blow with his pickax warns Remigio that it is not a good idea to be burying the girl this night. Although there is a strong wind, there are no trees with twigs to crackle as it goes by, no leaves to rustle, no obstacles to cause it to make a sound, nothing but branches of the avocado tree gently soughing. Accordingly, it is impossible to disguise the strokes of an implement necessary to make an opening in that stubborn, compact soil. You don't dig this ground, you break it, as they say in Icamole, and custom dictates making the fewest possible excavations because of an event in 1876, in which, after proclaiming the Plan of Tuxtepec to prohibit reelection, Porfirio Díaz rose up in arms against the government of President Lerdo de Tejada. His military campaign took off in the North, and finding invasion of Monterrey impossible, he proceeded in the desert as far as Icamole, where he had to face forces loyal to the federal government. Díaz suffered a resounding setback, and the seabed, covered with stones, some round, most with sharp edges, made conditions underfoot extremely difficult for flight, and the defeated soldiers foundered upon the many different thorny plants. Some historians relate that a large number of the bodies showed gunshot wounds in the back and nape of the neck and that Porfirio Díaz bewailed the annihilation of his army, thereby earning for himself the nickname of the Wailer of Icamole and the jeering of people who have no other pleasure in life than that of continuing the mockery year after year, since the Wailer was destined to regain his strength, smash his enemies, and have himself reelected president at will in a way nobody else was able to. However, those events that constitute a chapter of the country's history continue to be for Icamole an integral part of its present, inasmuch as every dead soldier was buried right where he fell, with neither cross nor gravestone nor bayonet nor flag nor coffin nor scapular nor flower nor X of stones nor emergent hand nor belt buckle nor broomstick nor erect member nor cactus marker nor letter to mother nor gold tooth nor glass eye nor obituary nor notification of death nor anything at all. Accordingly, there being no indication whatsoever in Icamole, it has become a common accident to find that, in excavating for a septic tank, foundation, or well, one is profaning one of those makeshift graves, in which case, a priest has to be called in, and the owner of the parcel becomes responsible for the expense of the new burial under a headstone without a name in the Villa de García cemetery, the only one authorized by the sanitation authorities in the region. For that reason, there have been no burials in Icamole since 1876, a custom from which Remigio is about to deviate.

He no longer wields the pickax; he sets it down and rakes it back and forth on the sandy surface. In any case, the sound is quite evident, mysterious even. Remigio decides to wait until the next day, when the sound of the impacts will be confused with that of footsteps, conversations, and the clatter of dishes, cutlery, and pots. He has only to be sure that at the moment he is carrying the body no boy is poking his head over the fence to ask for avocados the way Fatso Antúnez sometimes does.

He doesn't want to go into the house, is not sleepy at all, nor does he have any desire to be brooding the hours away under the same roof with the dead girl. Better to spend the night awake, to watch that nobody is spying on him, that nobody is jumping his wall. He thinks of Babette's pallor and wonders if her complexion was the same when she was vain and showing off her legs. He thinks of the panties the other way around, of making sure they are on properly, facing they way they should, and, in going about it, brushing accidentally against the little behind. No, Babette, you've got them on the wrong way around. Now I'll have to take them off so as to put them on again; and it turns out that, no, excuse me, I made a mistake, they were on right and now they are on the wrong way.

He goes to the tree and feels the avocados in the darkness until he finds the smoothest one; he strokes it. Babette, sad eyes, smile that once glowed; you no longer smile. He picks it and goes to the well to throw it in hard all the way to the bottom, to hear the sound of the splash and imagine a little voice saying, Here I am, Remigio, here, waiting for you.

The moon has moved halfway across the firmament when Remigio realizes that somebody is knocking. He picks up his machete before answering. Who's there? he asks. Lucio's voice is recognizable even though he is speaking in a whisper. Are you crazy? What are you doing up so late? Remigio opens the door with a sign to hurry in. Lucio is holding a book, which he hands to Remigio. Take this, it has the solution. Remigio sees the cover: *The Apple Tree*, by Alberto Santín. Light comes slanting in from the kitchen, the only room with the bulb on. He turns the book over to look at the back of the dust jacket. Fourth edition. A man tries at all costs to hide the crime he committed, but will be surprised when the victim finds a way to accuse him from the other world. Remigio drops the book on the dining room table. It's not a crime I want to hide, but a body.

Following this, the two men lock eyes in a prolonged stare. Remigio's say, I am innocent; Lucio's, however, are stern, not about to reveal anything. I placed a bookmark at the page you must read. There are almost 300 pages, and I am asking you to read only one, which I believe is a good offer. All right, but let's go out to the orchard. On the way Remigio picks up the kerosene lamp he had lowered into the well before. And to think that I was just about to withdraw this novel, says Lucio. It was saved by only one thing, that the hero's penis is small, and that seems remarkable to me; usually, writers like to see themselves in their characters and speak of huge members, perfect lovers, and enormous erections. To me it's all the same, Remigio says, and opens the book at the bookmark. Begin here. Lucio points to the second paragraph on the odd-numbered page. He knew that without a corpse there was no crime, and so no accused to bring to justice or, of course, a prison in which to serve a sentence under the suffocating conditions in those Veracruz dungeons where, it goes without saying, no prisoner, macho though he may be, doesn't end up weeping in repentance. Have pity, have mercy, I didn't do anything is to be heard, they say, in those cellblocks, which recall the imprisonments of other centuries, when judges were more severe, torture was practiced as morally desirable, and killing was done in the name of God. Remigio shifts his gaze from the book to Lucio. If what you are trying to do is scare me, you are succeeding. Pay no intention to that. Maybe I should ask you to begin further along, but you know me by now, and I like the way the church is criticized. Go on, continue. He pushed the little body with the toe of his boot and repeated with satisfaction, There will be no corpse, there will never be one. Then he smiled with a smirk that, if seen by anybody, he would swear was a smile of Lucifer. Once more Remigio left off reading. I am willing to accept that Babette and the girl in the kitchen are the same person, but now they are comparing this man with the devil. That is nonsense on Santín's part; nobody can swear that it is the devil's smile, because nobody has ever seen him smile or not smile. It is a dramatic and useless device, but that has nothing to do with you. Have patience and keep going. He grasped the wretched body by the hair and pulled it to the foot of the apple tree. Then he leaned over, felt the roots, and imagined how they would be arranged underground. He selected a spot two meters from the trunk at which to begin digging. He made a deep ditch so that his head barely emerged and went on to complete a tunnel directed toward the tangled heart of the apple tree's roots. He then pushed the boy's body into that tunnel until it was jammed between thirsty roots, roots that would encircle it like a boa, like honeysuckle, and devour every atom of flesh more voraciously than beasts of the jungle. That is a boy, Remigio says, pointing specifically to the word. I know, replies Lucio, and this is an avocado tree.

A pair of rural policemen arrive in the morning. These *rurales* ask questions here and there, but nothing suggests an official investigation. Perhaps they are there merely to intimidate with their khaki uniforms and gleaming .45s flaunted in heavy ammunition belts. Each wears a bandana around his neck, removed from time to time to dry a sweaty forehead, their cowboy hats pushed back but never off even when addressing an old lady. Seen a girl hereabouts? Anything suspicious? Out of the ordinary? Any stranger? A cry in the night? Questions are asked in a commanding voice and replied to negatively in all cases by fearful Icamole people. The *rurales* knock on no doors, interrogate only those stopped on the street, and wind up put out that nobody has offered them anything to eat or drink. We'll be back, they say out of vanity, out of embarrassment at having to go back empty-handed and without the slightest idea of how to conduct a proper investigation. They take off in a pickup truck the same color as their uniforms, pointlessly setting off a siren for the benefit of ants on the road.

And it so happens that red ants and cockroaches have begun to proliferate with particular ferocity. Some say that something in the drought is favoring their reproduction; others maintain that they have always been there as underground creatures that appear only at night, but that there comes a moment when they must surface to find nourishment, even at risk from the sun and of being stepped on. Lucio respects the ants for their will to create a place of their own; roaches, however, he detests for their opportunism in the way they storm any tube, cavern, hollow, channel, or pile of books. At the same time, he is prompted by that very contempt to hatch and feed them in the adjoining room into which he casts withdrawn books, considering this to be the ultimate indignity, which such books deserve to suffer. Burning seems to him an inappropriate form of punishment, for it confers upon an inane book the utility of producing heat, the distinction of being converted into light. Hell must be that which consumes slowly, between urinations and mandibles that tenaciously disintegrate book covers, dust jackets, authors' and authoresses' photographs with the intellectual pose of the former and the wishful beauty of the latter. The bugs have to regurgitate prizes, recognitions, and, particularly, bogus praise singling out each book as a consummate model of prose style, one of the great works of the genre, an example of impeccable literary quality, a masterpiece of the world of letters, he may enter the pantheon of great writers, the author's oeuvre in a class by itself, and so many other such efforts at pushing books that have no motor of their own. His mind dwells pleasurably upon the idea of a roach depositing its minute brown ovules upon a murky sentence of Soledad Artigas in which she explains that Margarita felt like a comet seeking beyond the firmament to land upon a planet that will take in an amorous sterile woman like her; or leaving its tiny turds upon characters like Raúl Sarabia, who, instead of dying with the dignity of a Josep Trovich or a Basualdo Fornes, expires while lecturing on history, philosophy, and sanctimonious love of Mexico. And he desires this novel to suddenly close, squashing the hapless cockroach, causing it to discharge its yellowish lymph upon some of those perfectly crafted dialogues, like, If you will allow me, Licenciado Sarabia, I must tell you, nevertheless, that, despite your curious interest in Señorita Carrington, your duty is, first and foremost, to your native land, for which you will understand, and undoubtedly be in agreement with . . . and so the death of that squashed pest, would seem a work of art among so much insipid verbiage. Some time before, Lucio had conducted an experiment: while reading *Sleepless Eyes*, he smeared honey with a tiny paintbrush on parentheses and dashes which certain authors use so widely for the purpose of subordinating or complicating sentences. To Lucio, those symbols are concessions provided by grammar to inept writers unable to discover how to link sentences together smoothly, in a natural way. He stapled a string to the book's spine and lowered it into hell. A month later he pulled it up. To his disappointment he found that the roaches showed no preference for the honey since they had consumed dashes, parentheses, bad prose and well-distilled sentences alike. He then accepted it as a natural thing, since the cockroaches had no cause to differentiate what the mass of readers does not distinguish.

Today, Lucio has another book for that hell, another sample of Spanish guile, *The Truth about Lovers*, by Ricardo Andrade Berenguer, man of letters, critic, journalist, musicologist, and film director, who considers the manner in which the protagonist extends his cigarette toward an ashtray, how the smoke spirals upward, and the sound of the jazz background music to be more important than actually revealing a truth about lovers. He goes to the door and pulls the little curtain aside. He listens to the bugs' mandibles munching the paper.

Remigio comes in with a basket full of avocados, which he puts on the floor. Some look ripe, others were picked too soon. Alberto Santín is an idiot who surely just imagined things and imagined them wrong; he never in his life dug a ditch or a tunnel, and it is obvious that he never buried anybody. How easy the way he tells it: dig hole, make tunnel, put boy in, and mission accomplished. But there's nothing more complicated than putting a girl through a narrow tunnel. If you push her by the legs, the knees bend; if you turn her around and push her by the head, everything bends. I had to put her onto a board and shove her slowly forward because, in addition, the tunnel was showing signs of collapsing. Getting the board out was another struggle, and the thing is that pulling on it too fast will make it come out, girl and all. I shoved it back and forth, and little by little the body stayed in place while the board slipped out. I probably drove a few splinters into her, but finally the girl was entangled in the roots of the avocado tree. I threw light on the tunnel but couldn't see much: the sole of a shoe, one foot with a sock halfway down the heel, the skirt all bunched up, her left hand. Now what? Do you think Santín explains how such a tunnel is closed up? No; the chapter ended and on to other things. You know how difficult it is to pack dirt down from above to below. Now imagine tamping sideways. At the beginning I was taking handfuls of dirt and throwing them in as hard as I could. Then I tied a ladle from the kitchen onto a broomstick; I filled it with dirt, pushed it as far as it would go, and turned it over. I had to repeat this thousands of times, and even that way I'm not sure the earth is going to be compact; a depression that runs from the main hole to the roots could appear at any point. When I finished I had a lot of dirt left over, enough to fill a bucket a number of times, which had to be scattered around the orchard. What was Santín's little dead body like? Read the novel and you'll find out. Maybe I will, but for now tell me what it was like. Lucio recollects for a few moments. Thirteen years old, dark, orphan, school uniform, close haircut. My girl was beautiful and never shut her right eye, even with the first scoop of sand I threw on her. Although I am never going to write it, I can imagine how the grains of sand from the ladlefuls that I spilled over her face stuck to her retina, how they entered the nostrils, the half-open mouth. Alberto Santín has always been unimaginative, Lucio confirms. He could never have conceived of a girl's body on the bottom of the earth, which is the bottom of the sea, among seashells and snails and trilobites, and age-old waves, among jellyfish that stroke her legs and currents that will tear her from the roots under your avocado tree and carry her off to an octopus den, where she will be embraced as not even her own mother did. That doesn't matter to me; all I would ask for is that the next time, instead of a novel, you bring me a grave-digger's manual. Judging by all the avocados you brought, Santín wasn't so far off the mark. And in view of the question in Remigio's eyes, Lucio goes on. His character picks all the apples as soon as he has the boy buried. And then? Remigio asks; the back cover says that things turned out badly for him. Yes, all the apples that later grew on the tree had the boy's face on them; the murderer picks them and feeds them to the donkeys, but the apples keep coming out faster and faster all the time. One day the tree is bare and the next it is covered with big, ripe, accusatorial apples. Leave me alone, Esteban, yells the murderer, naming the boy, but Esteban continues to appear on the apples with a variety of expressions ranging from happiness to anger to sadness. One night he decides to try something: to eat one of the apples. He chooses one that seems to have a serious expression, the eyes half-shut. He looks at it for a long time during which he strives to summon up courage to take the first bite. He cannot. He goes off with the apple to a bar and, when he is quite drunk, starts talking to it. The other customers fall silent, listening in on the strange man's conversation with a piece of fruit. Forgive me, Esteban, what must I do for you to leave me alone? He pours himself another drink and puts the apple up to his ear. It is a lengthy scene lasting about ten pages in which even the boy's early childhood and the bartender's impressions are reviewed. Almost at the end of the chapter, the murderer yells, I killed Esteban Sifuentes, it was me, with my hands. Notify his parents, the police, a priest, because I want to confess everything, and he bursts into wild laughter, which is no longer of the devil but, as Santín says, of a deranged mind. Remigio raises his voice, Then why did you suggest that I do the same? Santín's stupidities; I assume you don't believe in avocados with an open eye. Lucio takes one out of the basket and bites into it. Santín kills the boy with a knife; he speaks of the horror on the lad's face, of his eyes big as saucers. He describes the scenes of violence the way writers usually do: they mention the blood and the horror, but you don't see either, which is why they pad out their descriptions with adjectives. Lucio raises his voice; he talks as though addressing a crowd: Where do writers learn to kill and to die? At the movies, where nobody dies the way people die? If they were to come to Icamole one day, I would give them a goat and put a knife in their hand to cut its throat with; that experience would let them know that to describe somebody's death implies more than injecting a text with a variety of synonyms for horror, anguish, and pain. Lucio flings the avocado seed out the door. That's why, if it isn't done correctly, it's best to skip the death, like in *The Death of Babette*. Laffitte avoids faked descriptions and so is more striking, more true to life. Right now, as you were telling me how you got rid of Babette you created better literature than Santín could ever dream of doing. If I were your editor, I would make only one change: I would tell you that sand could not stick to the retina because the retina is in the back of the eye, at most around the pupil, but that is a minor change. I liked your description so much that I will be thinking about it for a long while. Remigio snorts and crosses his arms. To me that is not a narrative, it is real life and not a matter merely of a moment. I will remember the burial of that girl all my life. Lucio places his hand on his shoulder. Retina has to be taken out, and the last thing you said, very crude. Snorting, crossing your arms, is not a very creative way of displaying anger. Better that you talk about other things, for instance, about what you are going to do when the police come to show you Babette's photograph and ask if you have seen her, or about how you would react if you found a new anthill right on top of the burial.

He has more ideas but cuts his speech short. Remigio has left.

The drought had reached an intolerable stage. There is practically nothing alive left that could be eaten: no dry plants, no snakes, hardly one that would let itself be caught, no birds flying by, just teasing, for what stupid creature would think of making a den, a nest, or building a house here? The time had come to eat insects or leave. If water doesn't keep faith with these parts, said Father Pascual, we have no call to keep faith with it. Better rootless than to go on suffering the misery of thirst. It is unfair that elsewhere people throw open their windows to welcome a breeze while we must shut them to keep out the dust. Some arrived on their own two legs, others were simply born here, but now nobody else will have to die in this town. Get your things, only what is worth taking, and let us leave; we will not be the first town God has asked to emigrate. All were soon gathered in the square, and Father Pascual gave the signal for the exodus to begin. Wait, he said to Don Melchor, who was leading a cow, the only animal in the village still alive, I do not believe it was the Lord's intention that you should keep what he has taken from the rest. Leave her here, lock her in your house, and turn a deaf ear to her mooing. Don Melchor did not agree but he obeyed. He led the cow through the front door, casting a farewell glance around those three rooms he had lived in for so many years, had raised a family in. Abandoning the cow left him with a hand free to carry away something else; he hesitated between the portrait of his departed and a statuette of the Virgin of Fatima. He chose his wife and crossed himself before the Virgin. Don't be offended. The thing is that I can buy a statuette like yours in any market, but it's no longer possible for me to get another portrait of my wife. And he hurried off to catch up with the rest. Standing on a mound, Father Pascual directed the evacuation like a general commanding his troops. Onward, he said, do not look back, let the strong help the weak, the women help the children. Finally, there was not a sound to be heard but the bellowing of the cow. Father Pascual raised his eyes and said, Yes, Lord, you created us in your image and likeness, but likeness is not equality, and you gave us voice when you did not grant yourself ears. We go, Lord, leaving without blame the temple we built in this place, with its crosses and altar, its pulpit and confessional, because it was not us who broke the pact. The people departed just like the procession leaving for the cemetery when Simón died, except that this time, although there was no coffin, everybody looked dead. Father Pascual raised the skirt of his cassock and pissed as copiously as his dehydrated body allowed. The stream trickled down the mound into the dusty street and there it was absorbed at once as though it had never existed. Those were the last waters that land would receive.

Lucio hears footsteps outside and stops his reading. A woman is explaining to her young son why he should not chew with his mouth open.

What are you still doing here? he shouts at them. You were supposed to be leaving with Father Pascual. The woman looks at him in surprise; the boy, frightened. They turn to continue on their way, and the moment their backs are to Lucio and his library, they burst out laughing.

The *rurales* return in the same pickup truck, this time with a superior. They park in the place Melquisedec usually stops his wagon to distribute the water, and while they are deciding where to begin their investigation, Doña Rosario, a senile old woman, approaches, holding out an empty jug to them. Without a word being exchanged, she realizes her mistake and walks away.

The procedure followed by the police is similar at each house: the chief greets with a wide smile, introduces himself as Lieutenant Aguilar, and enters a living room or kitchen, any bedroom, or, if such is the case, the one room in dwellings that have no more than four walls. He proceeds to launch a series of questions that have no purpose other than that of testing how nervous people get, since he doesn't expect anybody to come out with a yes, it was me, I've got her in my pantry. The main interest is noting the expression on the faces of the persons being questioned when shown a photograph of the girl and asked if they know her. Remaining outside, the two cops glance into houses through a doorway or window, draw their .45s as if to put a shine on them. One says, Hipólito, mine looks like it wants a little action. Both smile and tip their hats if a girl happens to be passing. Sometimes, the chief comes out satisfied and says, Let's go on to the next house; sometimes he comes out more satisfied and orders a thorough search to be made. In that case, voices are heard raised in protest, the scraping of furniture being moved, perhaps a plate or a glass being broken, and a commotion caused by whoever makes no distinction between a search and an upturning of indoors, yards, storerooms, and corrals. The chickens scatter without the cops having to bother to avoid trampling them; the goats look on, unconcerned.

Remigio runs to the orchard as soon as he learns of the procedure the investigation is following. If the police were to work in a straight line, he would be one of the last questioned, since his house is at the opposite end of Icamole, but he has no confidence in the geometric exactitude of the visitors. Lucio has already asked him to think about his interview with the police, and so he visualizes a scene in which he is before the police, his voice shaky, stammering, unable to maintain a calm appearance at the sight of the photograph. The intruders search the house and orchard; one of them checks the well and says, I thought nobody had any water. Word gets around, and the people insult him, call him a traitor. Or worse, the well with water in it might attract police attention; maybe they lower a man to check, and I have no idea what happened to the other shoe. Did you find the body? the lieutenant will shout down the well. No, chief, but there's something here that might be worth your having a look. He calms down for a moment; the cops are too fat to get down the well, but imagination gives him no peace. He thinks of a boy offering to go down; of Fatso Antúnez pointing a finger at him. He also thinks of either of the cops standing near the avocado tree; the ground gives under the weight and a crevice appears. Looks like somebody might have been digging, says the lieutenant sarcastically, and Remigio sees himself handcuffed, escorted to the patrol car, answering, I don't know to all questions about the girl.

Removing traces of water is simple but laborious. It has to be bailed out with the bucket and poured noiselessly on any thirsty spot on the ground, which will soak up all traces of moisture in a matter of seconds. Remigio figures he will have to go through the process between fifty and a hundred times and proposes to carefully check each bucketful for the shoe, a bracelet, or any other personal object that might incriminate him.

He spends a couple of hours at the task, nervously at first but calming down little by little as the minutes go by, the water level is lowered, and nobody knocks. He even has time to pour a couple of bucketfuls near the avocado tree and tamp down the ground over the impromptu burial. Drink, Babette, he says, don't you go drying up like Icamole. The bucket gathers barely a few swallows of water the last couple of times; impossible to empty the well totally, but now he can say it is only a puddle of useless, stagnant water with vermin and slimy stones.

Exhausted, he pours the last bit of water over his head and seeks shade under the tree bare of avocados. He misses them and regrets having given that basketful to Lucio. He likes to stroke the peel of the fruit of his tree; he wants a woman with skin like that, smooth and lustrous, lickable; a skin impossible in Icamole with so much sunshine, so much dry wind, so much work in the farmyards or on the hillsides gathering nettles. There are no soft hands left in Icamole, no delicate feet, no way to feel, brushing against another woman, the kind of sensation contact with Babette aroused in him. Impossible with other women. Sometimes he calls up the texture of Señora Robles's legs: flabby, rough, fuzzy on the thighs and hairy on the shins. Sometimes he thinks of Encarna's breasts: full, bouncy, the nipples nevertheless very rough, very pointy, two big chocolate squares. There is nothing like the smoothness of his avocados, for which reason, on some nights he throws a few in the bed and stretches out with them. He offers them caresses, flattery. They are lovers with supple hands and nibbleable breasts, disposable lovers, no name, no obligations, and no future, because they wake up squashed on the sheets after having sacrificed everything for love. The avocado was the fruit of temptation, without a doubt, although people like to believe it was the apple, an inept whore with a smooth skin but a rigid body, sticky, no discretion in biting, which gets old all at once and consorts with flies and other insects. He knows that his girl is better off under the avocado tree than Santín's boy under the apple tree. He did not mention it to Lucio, but Alberto Santín also seems like a damn fool to him because he buries the boy without caressing him. In Remigio's case, on the other hand, each time he pushed on the girl's body to guide it between the roots, he felt himself closer to her. Her dress bunched up, he had to straighten the neck, hold down her knees to keep them from bending, take her waist between his hands, dust off her forehead. In his effort to tell a story about apples with the face of a child, Santín never imagined that whoever buries the corpse of a child ends up loving it. It was a struggle for me not to remain in an embrace with that body under the earth, kissing it, talking to it, whispering songs to relieve the sadness. Alberto Santín will never know anything about that, because writing is not living, because neither is reading.

Remigio leaves the tree, goes to his bedroom, and drops, sweating, onto his bed.

He no longer thinks about the *rurales*. Anxiously, he awaits the next crop of avocados. His hands slide over the sheet and he speaks the name Babette.

Lucio watches through the window as the police go about their questioning. Like Remigio, he expects the knock on the door at any moment. He prefers leaving it wide open as a means of circumventing ceremonial greetings and politeness. This is a public building, he says to himself; they are free to walk in. If they are asking the questions, they are in charge; if they want to read, I give the orders: take a seat at a table, be quiet, and no gum chewing; it is forbidden to underline or write on a page; no wetting fingers to turn pages; don't dare to tear out a page, no dog-earing, use a bookmark; and God help anyone I catch smearing boogers on a book or under the tabletop. Years ago Lucio attended a statewide convention of librarians in Monterrey. He learned there of the variety of things that may be found between the pages of a book: pressed flowers and butterflies, bits of bitten-off fingernails, notes, love letters, addresses, and, particularly, food: beverage spills, grease spots, molasses, crumbs, mayonnaise, and sauces; as well as what was specified in the minutes of that meeting as nasal residue, for the removal of which it was recommended that each library acquire a small spatula. Finally, it was also noted that, although infrequently, some erotic novels were inseminated, something, according to the chief librarian, that is not accidental but provoked, since a book is not perused at the level of the gonads. Some were of the opinion that the reader should pay for damage to books; others argued that it should be considered a normal part of use. Although no agreement was reached, debate ended when an elderly librarian asked how it was possible to ask a lady to refrain from wetting with her tears the pages of *The Sealed Window*. Lucio remained silent at all times; he was concerned about dust and the passage of time, not his nonexistent readers.

He goes to the bookshelf and takes down *City without Children*. Lucio enjoys the story of the ancient walled city of huge churches and castles that Paolo Lucarelli traces back to some distant century. Despite its remoteness in time, he feels it to be closer to Icamole than any other recent writing, inasmuch as the words used for the ordinary people seem to describe those who wander around the library: people who ride horseback, use wagons or walk barefooted; people who fix their meals with their own hands, who wring a chicken's neck. The clothing is different, and there are no palaces in Icamole, but Lucarelli brings an everyday touch to activities recent authors like to make grotesque or heroic, such as cutting up a steer or sleeping out in the open. Besides, he feels comfortable with dead authors because they describe objects without catering to the consumerism of readers. The sentence: Before going out, Robert put on his Giorgio Belli, the black one, Emily's favorite, sufficed for Lucio to withdraw *Mirrors of Life* without taking the time to determine whether it was a jacket or a hat that Robert had put on. Seems to him that a novel is less soiled by a reader eating over it than when the author mentions the brand of trousers a character is wearing or of his toilet water, eyeglasses, necktie, or the label of the French wine he is drinking in this or that restaurant; the mere mention of a credit card, automobile, or television set besmirches a novel. He detests automobiles because Detective Castelli doesn't get into his own car to drive from his office to the crime scene but, rather, to enable the author to spend time telling us about the traffic, the lights, the shops on the avenue and the songs playing on the radio. While waiting for the light to change, Castelli takes in the underwear model on the panoramic billboard and recalls the woman he met the night before in a bar. By the time he accelerates, he already has an enormous erection. That is why Lucio considers Icamole sullied by the pickup truck of the *rurales* parked where Melquisedec's wagon should be; it is inevitable to consider whether the vehicle is of a certain make, has a radio and a sunroof, if the occupants are wearing dark glasses of a particular designer.

He waits for almost an hour, reading parts of *City without Children*, underlining what he considers most significant in order to keep from losing the thread. He looks up hungrily a couple of times at Remigio's gift basket of avocados; but, bad enough that he is underlining that book, he is not about to risk soiling it like any youngster reading at a dining room table.

Lieutenant Aguilar arrives late in the afternoon. He shuffles briefly in silence before the bookshelves, the grit on his soles making a sound like sandpaper. Glancing around the room, he says, A *biblioteca* in this place, or should I be saying, a *bibliote*, followed by a guffaw. In the hope of making him feel uncomfortable, Lucio responds with a blank look. You got no clinic but you got books. Who can figure out this government. Lucio, at his desk, forces a smile although he feels like telling him, Get out because on account of you I broke a rule and underlined a book. He decides not to get up and greet him, for on his scale of hierarchical values a librarian outranks a law enforcement officer. The cop, obviously fed up and certainly annoyed, approaches with the photograph he has displayed so many times. Barely half the Icamole population has been covered in the day's interviewing, and he will have to spend the night here. He has no choice; returning to Villa de García will get him a reprimand from his superior. You've put everybody on alert, you fool, they'll get rid of the girl this very night, for sure, dump her on some hill or in the desert. Know her? Lucio leans forward, eyes glued to the image. Yes, her name is Babette. Lieutenant Aguilar pulls a chair up to the desk and sits. No, Señor, her name is Anamari, and we are searching for her. Lucio shrugs and looks up. Anamari, Babette, just names. The lieutenant takes out a notebook and writes *Vabet*. No, Lucio protests, it's spelled with B as in *burro*, double T and an E. The lieutenant scratches out, rewrites, and asks if it is now correct. Lucio reaches for the notebook. He would like to glance at the day's notes but is able to make out only Señora Urdaneta's name in ink that has bled through from the previous page. The two cops can be heard outside, one of them hawking and spitting. Do you have information on her? Aguilar turns to look around the room, his eyes resting momentarily on the door with the rusty latch. Lucio knows he should not wait any longer. He has no faith in this lieutenant's ability to comprehend but, in any case, is determined to test it, and so begins to read aloud from the passages he has underscored. Nothing is known about that man. He was seen to be living in the house that belonged to Guido Buonafalce before his death during the last flooding of the Arno. And nobody ventured to question whether it was an illegal occupation or if the modest dwelling had been inherited. His slovenly appearance, deep wrinkles, the ugliness of his old age frightened children or, at the very least, repelled them. As a consequence, a group of them invented a story about him: the old man had arrived together with the mud and debris deposited by the Arno; he had power over its waters and, if provoked, could call up another flood at will. Lucio purses his lips. It would have been enough to read the bit about the old man's disagreeable appearance, for mentioning rivers and floods in this desert would only confuse Lieutenant Aguilar. Although the children never believed their own story at any time, it amused them because they would yell at him and run off every time the old man appeared on the street. As time went by, the game evolved and became rather more aggressive; there was now an enemy to confront, to destroy. And so the old man was unable to leave Señor Buonafalce's former home without being assailed by insults and threats and an occasional mud pie. He skipped four pages and continued reading the next underlined section. The old man lost his mind, or at least that is what the people were thinking, because he would fill a large box with dirt, cart it in his wagon to a point in the Arno several leagues away where it flowed most furiously, and empty it into the water there. When he reached the city walls, the guards would dig around in the dirt, stabbing their spears into it. After a time, they got tired of checking. All right, old man, go on through once and for all and stop wasting our time with these loads of dirt of yours; and they ended chiming in with the mockery of the boys, who insisted that the dirt was meant to fill up the riverbed and cause another flood. Once again, the image of a raging river, but what can I do? *Pink Stockings* is about a gang of traffickers in children. Something too involved for these cops; and if I had tried *The Telegrapher's Daughter*, I might have set them right onto Remigio. Having lost his place he flips quickly through the pages. You are crazy, the guards told the old man, you couldn't ever make the river overflow with a million boxfuls of dirt like those. He turns two pages ahead and continues. One day, Benedetta, a daughter of the Spadas, went missing; another day, Luigi, the lad who helped out at the bakery. Finally, Marina's desperate mother, on the street screaming, Where is my daughter? A search was organized all over the city, since the guards guaranteed that nothing had passed the gates. A week went by in the course of which two more children disappeared. The authorities, unable to provide security, decided to issue an edict that forbade any child under twelve years of age from going anywhere outside the home unless bound to the father, mother, or guardian. Lucio knows that this book has whetted his appetite: there was no reason for having underlined that last sentence; it will only serve to distract Lieutenant Aguilar, provoking him to imagine children tied or chained by the wrist or waist as Murdoch and Tom did to drag Negroes. However, here is where his favorite part comes in: parents going off to work in the fields or shops with their children attached to them. The widower Antonelli takes nine offspring with him like beads on a necklace; Señora Perassi goes out with her fifteen-year-old daughter tied to her waist, who, in turn, has her own baby tied to her waist with a cotton sash. The girl protests because she is too old to obey the edict, but Señora Perassi shuts her up with a slap in the face. And that's how it is for a time. But when the adults tire, the children, rather than go out tied up, simply don't go out at all anymore, and the city becomes a place in pain, shut down, without light. And the old man continues his trips back and forth with his box of dirt, full on the way out, empty on the return, and they continue saying, Poor crazy old man, but behind his back. No longer does anybody want to make fun of him; they think of the children who never came back, the dead turned to dust, in that earth poured into the Arno, in a flood that will end up wiping out everybody. Lucio shuts the book with a bang, as if a fly had lit on its pages. What are you trying to tell me? The lieutenant stands up, and his tone of voice brings the two policemen in. Wait outside, he orders, and shuts the door behind them. What are you trying to tell me? Nothing, Señor, I was just reading. The book lies closed, Lucio's hand resting on the cover, concealing the title and author's name. Lieutenant and librarian cross glances for a moment, one waiting for a sign of nervousness, the other desiring that the visitor understand and leave. Melquisedec's bell can be heard at that moment. The water arrives in Icamole, and the people begin the trek to the wagon with jugs and pails in hand. I hope your information is trustworthy, the lieutenant says, or I'll be back for you. He leaves the library and waits a moment for his eyes to accommodate to the outside light; he traces the sound of the bell and reaches the rickety wagon with the drums of water. Let's take that man in, he says to the cops, pointing at Melquisedec, and they wait until he finishes distributing the water. Not until then does Lucio realize that the reading was perfect, that Melquisedec has Arno River water in his drums.

After the Battle of Icamole of 1876 ended and Porfirio Díaz had wept, after the chasing down and slaughter of people, and the yelling and the coups de grâce and disgrace when an enemy turned up wounded, the victorious army retired before evening, having found no reason for posting a detachment or even a couple of sentries to keep an eye on the newly conquered territory. What for? wrote General Fuero in a military report. Am I supposed to waste my brave troops on the protection of some stones and bushes, of nothing when it comes down to it? The inhabitants of Icamole did not poke their heads out until the smell of gunpowder had faded; they emerged from their houses asking themselves what the hell had happened inasmuch as day had dawned like most any other morning in the month of May. And when some people noticed columns of dust in the east and west, it was assumed that they had been stirred up by the wind; it was unimaginable until the guns went off that the cause was a couple of armies about to clash, at which point, men, women, and children raced back home with goats, chickens, and mules to safety from a stray bullet, an idle bayonet looking for work, a soldier with more libido than patriotism. It was not out of cowardice that we decided to hide under the bed or behind the wardrobe, Icamole men were to explain; the thing was that one can't choose which side to support if nobody explains why they are fighting. The village itself was not the center of the battle, so it suffered no major damage other than that caused by restless animals kicking at a building; there were scarcely any complaints regarding the victorious army's demands to be fed and allowed to use the outhouses, but the troops behaved in a very civilized manner and limited purloining to the boots, weapons, and personal belongings of fallen soldiers; there was no looting of homes, nor were women violated, to the good luck of some and the disappointment of a few others. Of course not, Lucio was to say over a hundred years later, with females like those, who would want to. But Icamole women told, rather, of dauntless wives, grannies, and virgins who had safeguarded their honor tooth and nail, not with tears, like Porfirio Díaz. And, as time passed, once involved in making up legends, they changed so many aspects of the battle that they turned it into a different one with other adversaries at a much later date, when Don Porfirio was no longer even in Mexico.

Days of hard work followed in Icamole, for it was necessary to bury dozens of the fallen. The men dug graves while the women searched for bodies. Since the men's task took longer and they calculated that at least five days would be needed to bury them all, when the women found a body, they emptied a tub of goat manure over it to keep ravenous beasts away.

For each dead soldier in turn they repeated the same procedure: he was picked up by the armpits and ankles in order to shake off the manure, deposited in his grave, somebody said an Our Father, the grave was filled in, task finished, and on to the next.

Precisely on the fifth day, when it was believed that the job had been done, a woman reported seeing a swarm of flies on a hillside. They found the body of a soldier there in the bushes, swarming with ants, face down, a bullet wound in his back. Obviously, General Fuero's men had bypassed him, because his rifle was at his left side and he still had his uniform and boots on; besides, said one of the bystanders, this boy hasn't been dead for five days, maybe a day, if that long. I'll take the boots, said another, but the rest looked at him disapprovingly.

On turning him over, they noted that the face was intact except for the eyeballs, because red ants, which prefer the softer parts, had already done away with them, and the speed with which they moved in and out of the nostrils indicated that they had taken up residence inside the corpse. There was a drained canteen under his belly and a letter addressed to Evangelina in his shirt pocket. It contained a declaration of his love for her, described the torture of nights with a bullet in the spine, and, guided by the spirit of one who was devoting his life for a cause, concluded with the assurance that the Battle of Icamole would be remembered by Mexicans for centuries of centuries, that the twentieth of May would appear in red on calendars and the fallen would be celebrated way up at the top of the nation's heroic pages. He could not imagine that many years later the history books would leave that battle out or, if at all, refer to it as a skirmish of no significance, books that, in any case, the Icamole people would never read.

The letter ended with Pedro Montes's signature but no indication of how to reach Evangelina; and there was no way to initiate a search because the dead man carried no documents. The soldier Montes was buried without the letter, and his was the only grave that was marked with a cross in case Evangelina should come forward or could be located. In time, the letter became an icon of veneration inasmuch as the word *love* is mentioned in it three times, twice as love for God and once for the Archangel Gabriel. In addition, it contained such phrases as the love I always professed for you and our children; because I know that one day we will see each other in the heavenly land; and you taught me to pray, and now with my life ending, all that remains for me is to do so, faithfull like a child. For that reason, with the passage of the years, the cross was transformed into an altar, and with the passage of more years, it turned into a chapel and became the closest thing to a church Icamole ever had: the chapel of the Archangel Gabriel where the letter is kept in a glass jar, where that afternoon, as in every after-noon of that month, a number of people will gather to pray for rain.

Now there is a double motive for coming together: they will also beg with the faith of Pedro Montes for Melquisedec to be fully cleared of his problem with the *rurales* so that they might soon have him back in Icamole bringing them water from Villa de García.

Lucio pokes about in the ground with the toe of his shoe until he uncovers a primordial snail shell, picks it up, and throws it as far as he can. Remigio watches him impatiently, waiting for an answer. When the shell comes to rest out of sight, Lucio says, Don't worry, Melquisedec isn't going to involve you, not you or your well. They had arranged to meet at Haslinger's Peak, the place so named by Lucio because the view from the top of a hill there south of Icamole so closely resembled the one Fritz and Petra saw when they first arrived at the hamlet. You talk very sure of yourself, says Remigio, but remember how those cops operate. They'll drag everything out of him down to the last gasp; it won't take them more than a couple of hours. They'll begin with fake friendly questioning, calling him pal, giving him a slap on the back or the leg, putting him on notice that real soon that same hand will be feeling a lot heavier. What do you say, my friend, you're going to give us the whole story, right? And maybe the pickup truck they were taking him in doesn't even get to Villa de García; maybe it stops in some out-of-the-way spot because all those vehicles carry a toolbox with hammers, pliers, screwdrivers, wrenches, jumper cables; and even if they didn't, there's stones, cactuses, thistles, and anthills. I don't see Melquisedec as having the guts to hold out against the *rurales*. They say they're even worse than the state troopers. I don't know, you can't ever really tell what goes on, it's all rumors that come out, but two minutes after that old guy confesses, they'll have the whole force on my property shining lights down the well, looking at the bottom, saying, No, there's nothing down here, and Melquisedec will swear to them that it's where he threw the girl in. Couldn't you be mistaking which well, old man? No, señores, that's the one, Remigio's well, and he will say it so sincerely that the *rurales* are going to start looking my way, then comes the questioning, and the punching, and just like in *The Apple Tree* everything will go against me, with no need for the avocados to be coming out with a girl's face on them. You've been reading it? I'm over halfway through, Remigio announces, and don't find it interesting or moving. Lucio picks up a stone that has a spiral etched on it. See this? This is an ammonite that died millions of years ago, yet we are still looking at it; it is the same size and shape as when it let itself be carried off by the waves and currents to hide from predators. Babette's evolution has begun. Your tree is surely going to turn very green with the twenty or thirty liters of water it will suck out of the body, and very soon, flesh, bone, dress, teeth, eyes, nails, everything will be absorbed. Your tree will swallow up in a little while what the sea and the desert would need centuries to cook. Tomorrow, the day after tomorrow, or next month, Babette will be an ammonite embedded in stone, and maybe some boy will find her and take her on the side of some highway to sell together with other stones, and whoever buys her will show her to his children and tell them about geological ages and cataclysms and oceans. Impossible that he will mention a girl named Babette, impossible also for the *rurales* to find her, because Melquisedec can't show them where she is, and if he tries, he will say whatever comes in to his head: she's on the notch up the hill, she's in the gully, in the missionary's cave, in the

66 ||

ravine of the hawks. And when he feels the pliers crushing his tes-
ticles, he will swear by his dead mother that he has her under the
mattress at home, locked away in the wardrobe, that he baked her
in the oven with onions, with nopals, that he lost her on a bet or in
a maze. You tell me, Melquisedec will beg them, you tell me what I
did with that girl.

A few people have gathered in the chapel at the foot of the hill.
Lucio points in their direction. They pray for rain but it doesn't
rain; they pray for Melquisedec but the *rurales* squeeze a little
harder. They'd do better to shut up, get their things together, and
leave Icamole.

The two men start home. Don't be nervous, Lucio says; if Zimbrowski's father doesn't give you away, nobody will. When they
reach the library they part with a nod.

A woman enters all in black, wearing dark glasses. She strolls about the library taking short steps, not clicking her high heels; stockings on despite the heat; bobbed hair; handbag of either leather or vinyl, Lucio is unable to determine which, but from the look of her, most likely leather. He supposes that a writer would name the exclusive shop where it was purchased, proving to his readers that he is no second-class hack but a refined author who keeps abreast of fashion whether in handbags or literature. The woman stops before one of the bookcases, hands clasped behind her back, and begins to examine the volumes, tilting her head to the left when title and author run up the spine, and to the right when they run down. The library is not brightly lit, and Lucio wonders whether she is really able to tell one book from another through her dark glasses, or whether she is trying to give the impression of being an intellectual, in which case, he prefers the frankness of Icamole women, who will not hesitate to bare their teeth in expression of their contempt for books. Lucio gets up and sits down again; he supposes he should say something, proffer a greeting, ask if she is looking for a particular title, but doesn't want to cut short the time he can watch her with her back to him, the sidewise movements of her head on the delicate neck, her arms with prominent bones, the way she rests her weight on one leg then the other, and the faint creaking of her knees. The moment will come to observe her from in front, to study her breasts, determine whether her abdomen is flat or bulgy. Seeing her kneel to examine the books on the bottom shelf, Lucio knows he will be spending the night thinking about her and the unfairness of this apparition of beauty in the village, unfair to a man who will have to turn out the light in order to turn on in his mind the swaying of the neck and the unrolling of the stockings over white limbs practically free of varicose veins shimmering in the moonlight that filters through the window; and then, after hovering a long time around his bed, he will make do with a few lines from *Rebecca in the Afternoons* the moment she slips naked between the sheets except for having kept her stockings on. Will you love me all your life? Rebecca will ask, and Lucio, after deciding to close his eyes and not open them again until morning, will answer, That's easy, Rebecca, for so little life we have.

The woman takes her glasses off, puts them into her handbag, and approaches the librarian. You mentioned Babette's name to the police. Lucio is accustomed to dealing with fat, illiterate women and does not know how to frame a coherent reply adequate for a woman with such slender hands. He wants to take them in his. I am Anamari's mother, the mother of the girl you called Babette. Lieutenant Aguilar told me you corrected his spelling. Yes, Señora . . . Lucio begins to frame his sentences; he thinks of the strange woman's black dress. He has heard that she is a widow, but doesn't know whether she is in mourning for her husband, her daughter, or simply likes wearing that color. No need for you to explain, the woman says, I am quite familiar with Pierre Laffitte's novel. It is a favorite of mine, and I realized long ago how great the similarity was between my daughter and Babette, not only physically, but in other ways. Do you remember the moment when her uncle André gives her the umbrella? Of course, Lucio says. Babette refuses it, saying that if anybody doesn't want to get wet, that person should stay home, but if they go outdoors . . . Thank you, Uncle André, the woman interrupts, quoting from memory. A ceiling protects against the rain when at home, but if the ceiling is the sky, it is better to get wet. Lucio hurries to the bookshelves for his copy of *The Death of Babette*. It's not that I doubt you, he says, it's that I want to feel the pleasure of seeing what I just heard. In a moment or two, he finds Babette's exact words to Uncle André and runs through them to the echo of the woman's voice. If the ceiling is the sky, whispers Lucio. There is no need to read what follows: niece and uncle go to a bridge over the Seine, open the umbrella, and drop it in. It stays afloat for a few minutes as it is carried off toward the Cathedral of Notre Dame. Anamari was thinking the same thing, the woman goes on to say, and she mentions to him that in rainstorms, just like Babette, she used to come home wet. And there are still other coincidences. Slowly, the enthusiasm in her voice shifts to a melancholy tone: Anamari twisted her hair into little knots with her forefinger, she ground her teeth in her sleep, she drank milk sweetened with sugar. It can hardly be said that the birthmark was different: Anamari's was like a spot, not a petrified teardrop; but perhaps that is a difference of perception, a concession on Laffitte's part. Lucio notes that the woman is speaking in the past tense. You're not expecting her to come back, are you? The woman breathes in slowly, unobtrusively. Babette didn't come back, did she? Lucio shakes his head and says, Poor Babette, poor thing, bells and more bells, a country that believes it is free, a girl who has no beliefs, and he immediately regrets having mentioned that ending. However, he was carried away by the urge to demonstrate that he, too, could quote lines of the novel from memory, since it is in such tight situations that Lucio recognizes the true reader and not in poetry, for schools oblige pupils to memorize some poem or other; the verses become imprinted on the mind, and, so, even twenty or fifty years later, the former pupil will take advantage of any opportunity to recite them, be it in a bar or at a family gathering. But that, Lucio asserts, is not literature, but a vain display of memory. Excuse my presumption, he says, but I did not mean to imply that your daughter . . . The woman brushes her fingertips over her forehead. Those very words have been lurking in my mind since Anamari became Babette; you have no idea what that time has been like, always the fear that sooner or later I would lose her on the other side of a door, by act of a hand snatching her away; that is why I detest bells, crowds. She never knew it, but I would follow her everywhere. Anamari would leave the house, and a few moments later I would go after her; two or three times a night I would look at her asleep to make sure that she was still in her bed. I asked her teacher never to let her leave school unless I was there at the door to pick her up. And all for what? We came to spend a week in Villa de García, and I made the mistake of feeling safe in that place, of assuming that in those towns there are not as many evildoers as in the cities. And good-bye, Anamari, good-bye, Babette. The woman lowers her head for a time, then reaches out for the book. This is the very same edition as mine, she says. Be good enough to read me the first lines of Chapter 4. The book is back in Lucio's hand, open to the place the woman indicates. Babette could walk in the garden with her eyes closed; she was perfectly familiar with the cobblestone path, the exact spot where the rosebushes grew, the gladiolas . . . No, the woman stops him, read the paragraph that follows. She came over to her mother and kissed her. The kiss was cold, like everything Babette did. Her smile, the cast of her features, her frankness, and, above all, her gray eyes won her sympathy, the affection of all. She never had to make an effort to obtain anything in exchange, for which reason demonstrations of affection became mechanical acts, mere well-mannered transactions. Enough, the woman says, and covers the page with her hand. I loved Anamari, her voice turns cold like Babette's kiss; she was my daughter, I had to love her. But would you like to know something? Lucio assumes that the question does not call for a reply, yet the woman remains silent, looking at him intently. Tell me, Señora. She opens her handbag and takes out a box of white pills, round as pearls, as Ricardo Andrade Berenguer would say, round as the turns of my life in search of the love that never comes, as Soledad Artigas would say. Lucio gets up and serves her a glass of water; on setting it down on the desk just where the sun strikes, tiny particles are revealed circulating in the liquid. My son brought avocados; I would like to give you some, if I may. The woman feigns not having heard, and Lucio knows that it is for the best in response to a phrase whose only purpose was to fill a vacuum. She empties two pills into her palm, pops them into her mouth, and takes a few sips of the Villa de García water, clearly displaying the moment liquid and solid travel down her throat. I am going to say something only you will be able to understand. Now she shuts the pillbox, doing so slowly, with the evident purpose of allowing time to pass; she shakes the box like a rattle, glances at the label, and finally settles it carefully into her handbag. She does not speak immediately but lets her breath be heard as a faint whistle through her nose and be seen in the rise and fall of her chest. Lucio becomes impatient with such a prelude on the woman's part and thinks of that Spanish screenwriter who considers the manner in which the protagonist extends his cigarette toward an ashtray, how the smoke spirals upward, and the sound of the jazz background music to be more important than actually revealing a truth about lovers.

As soon as the dust cloud appears in the east, the people suspect it must be the pickup truck of the *rurales* on the way, a grayish cloud in the early-morning sun indicative of a vehicle traveling at high speed. Too fast to be driving back an innocent person, says Señor Hernández. They wouldn't be that considerate, Señora Treviño comments; they'd give him a slap on the back, so sorry, take a walk. Some kids shouting Here come the *rurales,* attract Remigio's attention, and he joins the group of onlookers. He estimates how far away the dust cloud is and figures them to be arriving in a few minutes; no time to start running. Where to? In that respect Icamole has remained unchanged since the age of the trilobites; over the sea or over the desert, escape is impossible. They are coming for somebody, the woman exclaims. God forbid they should take my Adolfo away, says another woman; he would never harm a soul. Remigio controls his impulse to spit back at the woman, to yell at her, I hope they do take your Adolfo, I hope they put handcuffs and leg irons on him, pull a bag over his head, throw him shirtless into the pickup truck, and take him away naked as a pig to the slaughterhouse. Remigio's fear has become transformed into rage at the very sight of Adolfo, just out of bed, huge belly bared, pulling strings of mucus from his sleepy eyes. I hope to God they do take that lousy Adolfo away.

The pickup truck comes into a view a kilometer away, where the road starts downhill to Icamole and the surface changes from dirt back to sand. The driver gradually reduces speed, leaving sufficient inertia to brake hard alongside Melquisedec's wagon, standing all alone. The mules, out of faithfulness or enjoyment of a day's rest, have remained where they were left the afternoon before. Remigio turns away as the two men get out of the car and stride rapidly over to the group of people. Which is Señor Marroquín's house? one of them asks. They are the same two policemen with their .45s. The people look at one another without answering, uneasy at the urgency of the *rurales*. Are you referring to Melquisedec? asks Señora Urdaneta, pointing to a house of adobe like all the others; white, like almost all. The men, each carrying a canvas bag, go there. It is hard to tell them apart: both tall and obese, straining the seams of their khaki uniforms; both with scraggly mustaches they have undoubtedly been cultivating for years. One of them tries the doorknob and kicks open the door. We want no snooping around, says the other, making shoo-fly motions with one hand. The group moves back a few steps but does not disperse.

Icamole people are not accustomed to entering each other's houses. Visiting is conducted outdoors, on the street. Chairs and tables are set out, and all eating or drinking or chatting or singing or remaining silent until time to leave is done in the open. Remigio has never been inside Melquisedec's house, but some nights, walking past it when the light was on he could see a wardrobe with broken mirrors, an armchair with a plastic cover, and the old man himself facedown on an ancient brass bed; on the floor, plates, glasses, and clothing, farm implements, junk. Remigio has had only a few conversations with him; the subject was always about a family long ago, the city of Monterrey, squares, avenues, tinsel, nothing to account for how the old man came to find himself alone in a scruffy village. Yes, buddy, Melquisedec told him one afternoon, my mother was very beautiful, I have a photo of her somewhere, we were in the park, I was just a little fellow, but I can remember very well how she squeezed my hand, the way she told me, Smile, don't be afraid. She came out smiling in it, but not me. For Remigio it was natural for him not to be smiling; a small boy is required to be unhappy when having a name like Melquisedec.

The *rurales* come out with the canvas bags bulging, and even though they make a rattling sound when thrown into the pickup truck, some are convinced that the girl is in one of them. Do you know if he has another house? A storehouse? A corral? asks one of the *rurales*, mopping his forehead with his bandana. No, Señor, somebody answers, he has nothing but his mules. Both cops get into their vehicle and take off in a cloud of dust. Who's going to bring us water now? a woman asks. Nobody ventures an answer and all go about their business.

The door to Melquisedec's house remains open. The wind that night will make it bang.

It's going to rain sooner or later, Lucio says, because the rainy season is coming, because of the humidity, the winds, and the atmospheric pressure, because, finally, clouds will come that can clear Friar's Hill while still full enough without having spilled everything over Villa de García. And the people will be praising the Lord instead of complaining to Him about all the months of neglect. But, then again, that rain may make it here later rather than sooner, and by that time the inhabitants will be tired of waiting because of no water from clouds or Melquisedec, and so everybody will pick up their belongings and go off somewhere else, fed up with begging every year for the same reason. You will be leaving, too, one of these days, because your avocado tree has dried up, and I, finally all alone, will shut myself in my library so I can drown at the bottom of the sea.

The avocado tree has turned greener, Remigio says, and I have no intention of leaving Icamole.

Lucio's house is the only two-story building in Icamole. The library is on the ground floor, his living quarters on the upper floor, a single room that serves him as bedroom and kitchen, that's all, he needs no more. When he had the second floor built, communication between the two levels was by a ladder in the room of withdrawn books; after closing that access, he put in an outside stairway of stone. He likes to keep his home and library separate, to rattle his key ring every morning as he leaves. He no longer has a wife to say good-bye to, but mentally and sometimes aloud, he will say, So long, Herlinda, I'm off to work.

Lucio and Remigio, sitting on separate steps, watch the people getting into the buses. The church and township of Villa de García send them on Sunday mornings, the former to attract followers and donations and the latter to bring in votes. Families are usually loaded down with bundles of laundry and whatever they can sell in the market, mainly eggs, chickens, and goats. Now they are carrying empty jugs as well.

The buses depart at 9:15, leaving Icamole a defenseless village, but there was nothing to be defended against.

Lucio goes down the steps and stops in the street. The droning of the motors is lost, and it is unnecessary to raise one's voice to be heard. The woman took some pills, he says, probably to keep her courage up, and assured me that she hadn't even cried. She admitted to me that she felt relieved, not sad. What are you talking about? Remigio asks. Lucio looks at him in annoyance. He detests What are you talking about? an overworked device used by some writers for creating a dialogue when silence, leaving things implied, would be preferable. I don't know what you're talking about, Perkins says, and Inspector Fitzpatrick has to explain for the benefit of the readers, not for Perkins, how he discovered the guilty party by recounting about the fingerprints, the clues, and the contradictions. Madame Tursten had mentioned the locket, Fitzpatrick will say, and that indicated to me that if not the murderess she was at least a witness to the deed. You know very well what I'm talking about, says Lucio. Everybody saw the woman in black, followed her all the way to my library, all talking and whispering, and nobody took their eyes off her when she returned to her car and drove away. That's true, admitted Remigio, but the people are saying that she came to help you, that she is going to bring in more books, to pay you a salary, and to paint the front of your building; nobody mentioned anything about pills or not crying. Señora Urdaneta spoke to her before she started the car, asked her to roll down her window, and told her that Icamole needed water and medicine, not more books. I can understand a woman like Señora Urdaneta saying that; she thinks about medicine because her children have worms. But I expect something more from you; you've got something else on your mind. Remigio also steps down into the street. It takes a few moments for him to decide to speak, until he has erased the people's comments about the woman who came to Icamole to donate books. She loses her daughter and acts like nothing happened? Those are not my words or hers, Lucio says; besides, she is aware that the girl is not missing but dead. The woman has already been living with the grief for a long time; that's the reason she feels relieved. She knew that the girl everybody called Anamari was none other than her own Babette, who would have to be snatched from her by a mysterious hand and pulled in through a doorway. Nobody can feel relieved when a child dies, Remigio declares. If I were to hang myself from the avocado tree tomorrow, would you feel relieved? If the *rurales* were to come for me, would that make you happy? Lucio bursts out laughing. Anybody would think you've been reading gringo novels, he says; you talk just like one of those characters. Ever since Folsom died, the gringos have taken to writing melodramas about parents who are self-centered, addicts, or filled with obsessions, and children who suffer the consequences. An entire generation of writers busy running down their parents. Reason like a man, Remigio. You are living in Icamole, not an English-speaking suburb. They glare at one another briefly, unsure as to whether the next word is going to fire up a quarrel or make peace. A clap on the shoulder suffices to cool Remigio down. Come with me, Lucio says, there's something I've been wanting to do for some time, and he walks him over to the Archangel Gabriel chapel.

This is the first time we've been here together, says Remigio. Lucio smiles and points to a bare metal chair. Since you are in a sentimental mood, sit here. Remigio obeys, looking up questioningly. It was your mother's chair, Lucio explains, where she would sit sewing, chatting, dozing, and passing the time. Does it feel comfortable? Remigio doesn't answer; he thinks he didn't hear right.

A carpenter was never hired to build pews for the chapel, and the congregation, especially the women, were accustomed to bringing a chair of their own for ceremonies, whether a rosary, a prayer for rain, or a fiesta for the patron saint when the priest from a neighboring town was invited to celebrate Mass for just that one time each year. Carrying chairs back and forth got to be such a bother that the women took to leaving them in the chapel; that's why there is such an assortment of furniture: chairs of metal, plastic, rattan, folding chairs, straight ones, upholstered in a variety of colors and discolorations. Austerity is also the rule with respect to religious icons. On the right-hand wall hangs the cover of *Guadalupe Hymnal*, a novel by Héctor Lanzagorta, which an overzealous parishioner filched from Lucio's desk in the library on a visit to request a donation for the restoration of the chapel. Lucio never tried to recover it, since *Hymnal* was destined for the WITHDRAWN stamp, and he was glad that nobody had taken the time to read it and so to discover that it was a sacrilegious book, since the figure representing Juan Diego in adoration of the Virgin depicts the young man with a bulging crotch. On the wall to the left, a shelf upon which there sits the jar with the soldier Pedro Montes's letter inside, surrounded by four votive candles, three unlit, one burning. It is of clear glass narrower at the top, where the cover is, but slightly wider, in fact, than at its base. Lucio and Remigio approach. I always thought the jar originally held peaches in syrup, Lucio remarks. The paper is exhibited by being pasted to the glass inside the jar, which acts as a showcase, enabling Evangelina's letter to be read from beginning to end. I once tried taking the cover off, Lucio relates, but couldn't. I wanted to open it because Pedro Montes wrote the word *faithful* with a double l and in all these years nobody had realized it. Taking a red pen from his pocket, Lucio says that the time has now come to correct the error. Don't count on me for help, Remigio takes a step back; it is Icamole's most precious relic, and you have no right to do that. Lucio shakes his head, sits in a chair, and puts his hand on the chair next to it. Much more comfortable than your mother's. Remigio snorts and goes to it. He cannot recall his mother sitting in that chair or anywhere else. To him, whenever he thinks of her, she is always a standing figure with her back to him. Lucio closes his eyes and speaks unemotionally. If you were a gringo novelist, this would be your point of departure: the day my father induced me to participate in an underhanded act; and you will have pages enough for you to be sarcastic with me, to show me up before all your readers as a poor devil, whom you love in spite of everything because you yourself are a good person.

Remigio stands up, submissive, and thrusts his hands into his pockets.

They return to the jar, Lucio grips it between his hands as Remigio twists as hard as he can to loosen the cover. The first attempt fails. The air inside has been locked in since Don Porfirio's time, with the soldier's evaporated spit floating in it after he kissed the letter just before he died, and Can you think of anything more? You're the storyteller, Remigio says; all I know is that anybody who desecrates a relic is in for trouble. Lucio slides his palms over his trouser legs to dry the sweat. We're already in trouble and paying for it in advance. They make another attempt. This time Lucio has the jar in his armpit wedged between his arm and side. The cover gives with a sharp crack. Remigio turns it barely enough to loosen it. Lucio finishes the task, extracts the paper, and examines the sentence closely: You taught me to pray, and now with my life ending, all that remains for me is to do so, faithfull like a child. He draws a red circle around the double l; next he writes in parentheses with the same ink: faithful doesn't have a double l, although we should be full of faith. He replaces the letter, screws the cover back on, and asks Remigio to tighten it. Regarding the dead girl, you needed an ally; regarding the letter, I need you. He puts the jar back, takes a match from the shelf, and proceeds to light the three votive candles. Don't consider this a disrespectful act; on the contrary, Montes deserves my respect because, dying and stretched out on the stones, the only mistake he made was in one letter. Without doubt, he was a man of letters and, if he were alive today, he would be a frequent visitor to my library and my best friend.

They leave the chapel and head down the hill toward home. No matter that you are throwing it up to me about gringo novels, says Remigio, I still think there's something strange about that woman. She drives a dark, silent car; maybe she's the one who killed the girl. It's possible, Lucio replies, but even so, I wouldn't condemn her. I would have given her a hand myself in pulling the girl out of the trunk, carrying her in the dark, and throwing her down the well, although I would have liked it better if she had brought her on horseback, not in a car.

To Lucio she is not merely a woman standing with her back to him who had left her chair one day in the Archangel Gabriel chapel; she was a name to him, she was Herlinda, with a skin that beckoned, with a way of looking at him in the darkness and a voice that grew softer if he held her tight. To Lucio skin was of utmost importance in a woman, not its color, as in the novel by MacAllister, but its texture. That was why he married Herlinda when she was still practically a child and why he asked her not to do heavy work or to stay very long in the sun; she had to be shielded from turning into one of those Icamole women with calluses and hands like a man, body upholstered in leather. There's nothing like being able to snuggle up to smooth skin during the night. Memories of Herlinda well up often, and he is saddened that the most frequent one should be that of the two of them seated opposite each other at the table, about to eat a vegetable soup. She takes the first taste and makes a face, saying she put in too much salt. He takes a spoonful and, sure enough, the soup is inedible, but he holds back a grimace of displeasure and keeps eating: that's the least he can do for her. It tastes fine to me, he says, and so as to leave no doubt about it, he finishes his plateful and serves himself another. Nor does it seem to him a particularly tender remembrance or a laudable sentiment, but ever since Herlinda died it pops into his mind whenever he picks up a saltshaker, and it comes back to him in every detail: the slices of carrot and squash floating in seawater, the plastic tablecloth with the checkerboard design, a calendar for the month of March on the back wall. Herlinda in her green dress, arms crossed, downcast because of the wasted vegetables, her pregnancy about to explode, and asking, Do you think the goats would eat it? On some nights he calls up Herlinda nude, but Lucio prefers to avoid mixing desire with nostalgia and replaces the image of his wife with one of the heroine of *Rebecca in the Afternoons*. He expresses his love to Rebecca, as well, but without making pledges, in the knowledge that before daylight she will have returned once more to her daily life with Doctor Amundaray. Rebecca is very different from Herlinda; but Lucio enjoys her company, takes pleasure in her short, spare sentences, her walking about the house with nothing on but stockings, the certainty that she will be gone the moment desire wanes. Rebecca does not snore, pull the blanket off him, would never make a vegetable soup for him or plan for the future; nor would she even venture to mingle with the Icamole people. Rebecca is for occasional nights; he would have wanted Herlinda for his whole life.

It was Herlinda who brought the first book into that house: *Manual of Goat Husbandry*, which dealt with the raising, feeding, and butchering of those animals. The author asserted that, if goats were provided a happy environment, they would yield richer milk and better meat. They should not be treated as animals for slaughter, he said, but as pets, talking to them affectionately and patting them from time to time, giving them each a name, if possible, that should have a maximum of two syllables and, preferably, begin with a vowel. It is advisable to protect them at all costs from being frightened in the night by a coyote, and to prevent fighting between males, since nothing adversely affects the flavor of the meat so much as fear. Likewise, it is advisable to provide them balanced food beyond what usually grows in the pastures. Lucio was raising goats at the time, and Herlinda foresaw a way of increasing their flock and passing the knowledge on to neighbors so as to make Icamole an important livestock center. It is now no longer possible for us to expand, because this desert does not yield enough to feed more goats, she said, and for that reason the first step is for us to set up a storeroom in which to keep sacks of the balanced feeds the book mentions, the medicines for treating parasites, and additives for delaying the souring of the milk. Lucio put the matter off for so long that, when the second story of the house was finally built, freeing up the entire lower floor for use as a storeroom, Herlinda had already been dead for a number of years. One morning she said she didn't feel like getting up, that she had a sharp pain in her legs. Lucio went out to do the chores, and when he got home at dinnertime he found her still in bed. Touching her, feeling the change in her texture, was enough to impel him to draw the sheet over her face. He did not pray or have thoughts about the soul or life in the next world. He regarded the outline of the body and regretted not having made love to her the night before. Then he went to the door to wait for Remigio to come home from school. Knowing that he did not have the gumption to tell him the news directly, as soon as the boy was in the doorway, he said, I'll fix dinner myself today. He would let things take their usual course, would fulfill the obligations of a Mass and burial in Villa de García, and would wait until Remigio was sound asleep and then, yes, sit down and cry.

Since there was no certainty as to the cause of Herlinda's death, Icamole ended up accepting that it was because of a scorpion sting, and that was what eventually made Lucio continue the construction of the second floor. At one of the memorial anniversaries he spoke to Remigio about the unconsummated feed storeroom. Do you think it would have been a good business? I don't know, Remigio replied, but at least the scorpion wouldn't have gotten up to the second floor.

Lucio sold his goats that same day to raise the money for the construction, even though it was just a tribute to Herlinda's memory and would mean being left without a peso for the balanced feed recommended by the *Manual of Goat Husbandry*.

For that reason, when the state government agent arrived with a van full of books in search of somebody with extra space, the people took him to Lucio. The man entered the unrealized feed storeroom and nodded. Looks to me like plenty of space, he said, pointing around to various spots, the bookshelves over here, the desk over there, and in the center, the reading room. He offered Lucio the post of librarian and assured him that within the next few days a van would be there with shelving for the books. In view of Lucio's hesitancy, he mentioned salary and benefits and that he would be the only man in Icamole with a desk job. The agent took papers from his briefcase and held them out. As Lucio reached for them, the man drew back his hand. Can you read? he asked, the empty-house echo in his voice. Lucio didn't feel like taking offense and so merely nodded. While signing the original and three copies of the contract, he silently begged Herlinda's forgiveness for having abandoned the feeds project.

Sitting up naked in bed, elbows propped on his thighs, Remigio raises his head and tells himself that he doesn't want to spend the whole night that way. Loneliness was never his problem, but since Babette has been lying under the tree, his pillow has been unable to put him to sleep. Had he found her in the well alive, he would have had no hesitation in rescuing her. Hang on to the rope, girl, don't be afraid. And once out of the well, he would have handed her something to dry herself with. Here's a towel. Change your dress. I'll lend you a shirt. And he would have waited in the orchard for the girl to come out dried off; he would then have taken her by the hand to look for her mother. But she was dead when he found her, and from that day on his mind has been building up images: black hair, one eye that will not close, panties with the label properly in place, an arm that seizes Babette as bells ring, white skin, white thighs, flat tummy, lips half parted. For that reason he is now no longer the same and feels grateful that the *rurales* did not show him her photograph, he wouldn't have been able to withstand the sight of those gray eyes of when she was alive. That is why he is sure that, if he were to go to the well this very moment and find the girl alive, he would no longer have any inclination to give her back; it would be a matter of a minute or two to lay her down on the bed, even if it had to be by force and gagging her. Don't be afraid, girl, don't be afraid. Your mother has given you up as missing, as kidnapped, as dead, as a novel whose ending is in the title, as a bunch of pages that eventually call for a full stop. But there is a continuation to every story even if it remains unwritten, and what's next in yours? The door closes and what's next? The bells ring and what's next? Don't be afraid, answer me. What's next, Babette? Do you really like the story of a dead girl in a well? Or would you prefer it if somebody rescues you in time, if good old Remigio rescues you?

He pulls on trousers and goes out, barefooted, without a shirt. His first stop is at Melquisedec's door. Although there is no wind, he props it open with a stone to keep it from banging. Cautious in the darkness, he imagines himself the suspect who would fit in perfectly with the needs of the *rurales*, much better than Melquisedec, for whom they will have to invent a story that dovetails with his comings and goings in Villa de García as well as schedules, circumstances, and witnesses, with a squeaky wagon that never entered any town without being announced by the goat bell. It would be sufficient for the *rurales* to have posted a guard to check on him and say, He was out on the street in the middle of the night. He went into Melquisedec's house. The interrogation would then begin. What were you doing? Were you maybe concealing evidence? Where do you have the girl? Where? And Remigio would go to pieces without need for torture. I have her buried, he would say between sobs, and it would seem useless to him to be adding that he did not kill her, but maybe he would throw in that he did not touch her, not in the way they all would like to. Shirtless, handcuffed on a metal chair, he would be angry at himself for not having showed greater fortitude, and like a gringo novelist, he would blame Lucio, because he was never able to set him a good example, and he would explain to the *rurales* that he strayed off the straight and narrow on the day his father induced him to participate in an underhanded act.

He goes up the stairs at Lucio's house and taps gently on the window with a stone. He counts up to ten and, hearing no sounds inside, knocks louder. Lucio opens the door, a sheet wrapped around him. What do you want? What time is it? Remigio enters without answering, feels for the switch and turns on the light. He glances all around the room and shakes his head. Where are the avocados? Don't tell me you gave them to that woman. I want them back, I need them. Lucio goes back to bed and lies down, his eyes closed. If I don't throw you out, it's because I like you the way you now are, with that same distraught, violent attitude as Kartukov; although like this, with no shirt on, the Saint Petersburg winter would do you in. The avocados, insists Remigio, give them to me.

Observing the three women and two men in his library, Lucio feels let down. I thought more people would be interested in knowing what happened to Melquisedec, but I see that his fate, his life, doesn't seem to bring folks together the way the water did. Having set up twelve chairs in front of his desk in three rows of four, he is annoyed because the half-empty room gives the meeting an atmosphere of failure. What is more, the five persons present are over fifty; it is impossible to expect their minds to be alert, receptive to words.

At about noon that day, Lucio made the rounds of the houses in Icamole to notify people. At four in the afternoon, if you want to find out what happened to Melquisedec, he told hem, I'll be at my place expecting you. He did not wait for a yes or no, since he was not posing a question but extending an invitation. He had confidence in the curiosity of people and the affection they would feel for Melquisedec after he became the water carrier, after having thanked him every day for filling their receptacles, and if only twelve chairs had been set out, it was because he had no more and would never have agreed to holding the meeting in the chapel. It is four fifteen, he says, let us begin. He refrains from clearing his throat even though he feels it tickling, because people in run-of-the-mill novels always clear their throat before beginning to read.

They had pulled his shirt over his head, knotting the sleeves tightly over his eyes. Although he could hardly breathe, Melquisedec felt more suffocated by the heat than the wrapping. The vehicle sped over a dirt road, but he was seated between the two policemen, so none of the breeze reached him. On the other hand, it was comforting for him to think that if they had blindfolded him they were not planning to kill him. Why bother hiding the route from him, the destination, from somebody who is going to die? The driver shut off the motor and let the car roll to a stop. Here we are, one of them said. Where? asked Melquisedec in a muffled voice. He was answered by being yanked out of the car and shoved to his feet on the stony ground. The cop with onion on his breath untied the shirt. It was late afternoon and Melquisedec's eyes adjusted to the waning light. Where are we? You, go ahead and run off in that direction, said the one with the scar on his cheek, pointing, and if you reach that hill there you're free and can go home. Melquisedec was confused. He had heard of *ley fuga*, the right to shoot an escaping prisoner, but assumed it was an aspect of Mexico's legendary and barbaric past. That shots by that pair would miss was too much to expect. The hill was some 200 meters away, and Melquisedec's legs, old and frightened as he was, refused to respond. He imagined himself with two bullets in his back, dying, dumped in that pickup truck on its way back to town. He could hear one of the *rurales* talking to the chief: He tried to escape, we had to shoot. Okay, he would answer, but take him for another ride, he's still breathing. No, Señores, Melquisedec plucked up courage to speak, I won't do you that favor. And he began to walk backward toward the hill, always presenting his bare chest to the policemen. The old coot turned out to be pretty smart, one of them said. Should we shoot him like that? No, the other whispered, I have a better idea, and raising his voice, said, You win, let's get out of here. They climbed back into the vehicle and traveled on the dirt road to the highway, only the seating was changed. On the way back to town, Melquisedec was now next to the door, the wind stream generated by the vehicle traveling at a hundred kilometers an hour blowing on him. Responding to a wink, the cop with the scar on his cheek in quick succession pulled up the door lock button, opened the door, and began pushing Melquisedec out. His back braced against his companion, he began kicking the old man out, who, whimpering, begged for a mercy that was not en route on the highway this night. Take pity, have mercy, I didn't do anything. The last syllable elongated into an extended scream when the cops could only see one of Melquisedec's hands still clutching the door frame. Close it? one of them asked. No, wait and see how long he hangs on. It was barely a few seconds before the old man let go, finger by finger, no longer shrieking.

And how did you find that out? asks one of the women. Lucio looks up: he was considering reading up to the point where the car is shifted into reverse and the police confirm that Melquisedec is dead; however, that could remain implicit. He closes the book and holds it up for his audience to see. I know because it is written. The woman who had questioned him comes closer to read the title, *The Laws of Blood*, and verifies that it is an old book, the pages yellowing. So, then, it's a bunch of lies, she says on the way back to her seat.

No, Lucio shows the book. Eustacio is the name of the character in the novel. All I did was change it to Melquisedec; the rest is all true. The two men in the audience get up, say good-night, and leave; the three women remain seated, in silence. I also have another novel in which the townspeople meet in a library to find out what happened to a person arrested by the police. One of the women starts toward the door. I suppose that's where you got the idea to bring us together. One of these days you are going to know that Melquisedec was thrown out of a speeding pickup truck, and then you will be coming to the library to find out in a novel with whom your husbands are cheating on you, when your children will leave Icamole, or why the one who went to work across the border never came back, or if your daughters are still virgins, or if that idiot Fatso Antúnez has already knocked them up. Don't tell Señora Vargas, but I read in *The Black Frontier* that her husband never reached Chicago because he drowned in the Rio Grande without identity papers; that's why those who found him floating there took his clothes off and threw him back in. Or, if you prefer, tell her, so she can stop waiting for him. Listen, Lucio, with no need to look in your books, we all know that the police picked Melquisedec up as soon as they left your library. If the old man really did something to that girl, then let him rot in prison, but for a real reason, not one, let us hope, out of a novel. Pleased with her threat, the woman makes a sign to her companions and they exit.

Eustacio lay dead under a no-passing road sign. Better Melquisedec, also, Lucio says to himself, even if it happens to be a cattle-crossing sign.

Melquisedec's house is a shambles. The two sackfuls the *rurales* carried out bulging with God knows what made little difference. One would have to step carefully to avoid treading on an enamelware spoon, an empty green-sauce can, or bumping into an overturned armchair. The room feels stuffy despite the wide-open door. Remigio goes into the bedroom, a space barely large enough to accommodate a bed and wardrobe, one window gives onto the street, visible from the other, a watering trough and further back in the field, the two mules. The wardrobe's two drawers are open: in the upper one, a pair of socks, a box of toothpicks, a nail clipper, and two jockey shorts. The police certainly wouldn't have touched the underwear. Remigio supposes that Melquisedec changed underwear at intervals of three, days or weeks or whatever washing cycle the old man followed. One pair of shorts is red and the other, blue, both of the same type, purchased undoubtedly in a package of three, size medium. The pair he was wearing when they took him in must have been green. The police know the exact color now, he says to himself, and sits down on the woolen blanket on the bed. He closes the upper drawer so as to examine the contents of the other one. Trousers, a jar of ointment, a belt, and a large manila envelope tied up with a string. If I were the policeman, he says to himself, I would have thrown that envelope into one of the sacks or, at least, opened it. Could they have ignored it, or is Melquisedec already dead, and the cops only grabbed things at random to give the appearance of an official search. He picks up the envelope and begins to bite at the string; only then does he speculate that there might be incriminating evidence in it, and that the *rurales* themselves put it there so as to make another trip and say that here is the proof we needed. However, what such proof might consist of does not occur to him, so he continues gnawing on the string until it breaks. He sees sepia photographs in the envelope and pokes it under his belt without looking at them. He goes to the door and peeks out in both directions. The coast is clear, but before leaving he returns to the wardrobe, opens the upper drawer, and pockets the box of toothpicks.

Acquaintances in Monterrey call to tell me how sorry they are, that they will be praying for Anamari to be found. In Villa de García people don't talk to me, some look at me pityingly, others with satisfaction, serves her right, let the woman suffer. Then the *rurales* and the state police come and keep asking the same questions, Where did you last see her? Were you having any trouble with her? Do you know if she had a boyfriend? Do you suspect anybody? Did you get a ransom demand? And instead of them looking for evidence, they stare at my legs, and I tell them I know nothing. What would be the point of my telling them about Babette and Paris and the bells. I don't know anything, because if I tell them to go home, take it easy, drop the whole thing because Anamari is never coming back, then they'll think I'm guilty of something. I know nothing because they aren't interested in my daughter as a missing child torn from her home, but as a trophy; competing is all that matters to them, to see who finds her first, the state police or the *rurales*, and after all the questioning they don't even know where to begin and make excuses with that stupid remark about a needle in a haystack that is so common, even though nobody has ever lost a needle in a haystack and, in any case, hay can be set on fire and pretty soon a shiny needle will stand out in the ashes, or, it could be pulled out with a magnet. But setting the whole desert on fire to uncover the gleam in my daughter's eyes, the blackness of her hair, the whiteness of her belly button, is something they won't do and couldn't do, because finding Anamari is more complicated than that; they would have to question Pierre Laffitte to ask him to write a sequel to *The Death of Babette* and to lay out for us the interior of that mansion or palace or dungeon where the arm came out to snatch her from the pages and this world, an impossibility because the writer has been asleep for many years in the Montparnasse cemetery.

Don't worry, says Lucio, I will not be praying for your daughter or sympathizing with you or telling you how very sorry I am. That suits me fine, says the woman, in black again but now wearing a looser dress. I would prefer for us to read a book. Do you have *The Promised Parcel*? Lucio shakes his head. Too bad, she says, sitting on one of the twelve chairs, still arranged in three rows of four, today I feel like some light reading, a family saga in which the people are united, love one another, are honest and working the land. In which suspense is created when the eldest son brings his fiancée to the house or when the youngest comes down with a fever or when Helga, the only daughter, decides she wants to become an actress. Her father says, No, you would have to go to the city for that, and I don't know what dangers lurk there. And the mother shuts herself in to weep in silence because, twenty years earlier she, too, had dreams of becoming an actress, but her father forbade it. I would like a novel that tells of a life lived between sunshine and wintertime year after year, that speaks of good harvests and others devoured by pests, until the owner of the parcel is satisfied that all his children did something worthwhile with their life, since even Helga will one day bring him her newborn child and thank him for having prevented her from going off to the city.

Instead of holding your grandson in my arms, she will tell him, I would be a cabaret singer in the arms of a scoundrel. So the man will embrace his wife and remark how time flies, and she, for the first time in her life, will forget her dream of becoming an actress and respond to her husband with a kiss. I would like to read just the ending: the man and the woman embracing; it is snowing outside and inside a fire is burning in the fireplace. No, says Lucio, I don't have anything like that. He recalls two novels with a couple embracing; no snow in either, just a beach and cliffs, and the cockroaches finished off both. He points to sealed cartons in the corner. *The Promised Parcel* might possibly be there. Would you like for us to look? The woman goes to the cartons and examines them; the postmark shows that several have been there for more than five years.

I read the books one by one before deciding whether to put them on the shelves or to send them to hell. No need for you to explain, she says, there are always more books than life. Printers could have been on strike for the last ten years and nobody would notice. Did you know that out of every twenty-eight pages published, only one is read? Because books are given to people who don't read, because they land in a library that has no users, because they are obtained to fill up a bookcase, because they are given away with the purchase of some product, because the reader loses interest at the first chapter, because they never leave the printer's warehouse, because books are also acquired through impulse buying. I just finished getting rid of *Autumn in Madrid*, says Lucio. I was on page 63; that left 208 unread. I never got past page 20, she says. For a bore like that to reach Icamole calls for the connivance of an author, proofreaders, editors, printers, booksellers, and even readers, to say nothing of the writer's better-half, for her to say to him,

DAVID TOSCANA

Yes, darling, you sure know how to write. Organized larceny, he says. Smiling, they regard one another for a moment, Lucio yearning to shed thirty years or, at least, for things to be as in *Hidden Lives*. Have you read *Hidden Lives*? Didn't like it, she says. I believe that Miranda should have left the house the first time her husband struck her. Lucio is disappointed that the woman should reject such a masterpiece on the basis of a moral judgment; to be sure, they could sit around and argue over whether Miranda deserved the beatings or not, but that seems to him irrelevant. The point is that she decided to take the husband's abuse and, thanks to that, there is a novel worth writing. Thanks to that, there is a glorious scene in which Miranda shuts herself in the bathroom and molds a cake of soap into the shape of a penis, holds it out in front of her pubis, and deepens her voice to say, I cannot let it pass a second time. She goes into the shower and scrubs her body with the soap until it is all gone, then bursts into tears under the stream, exhausted, to wait for her husband to arrive. But Lucio knows that it is difficult for women to read amorally and that they cannot resist identifying with those of their gender. You think that Miranda should have left her husband, says Lucio, but you don't object to Babette's having knocked on that door. Decision is not the same as destiny, the woman replies. Miranda had options while Babette would have fallen into the hands of that mob. Lucio nods. *The Death of Babette* would have been ruined if, instead of bells and more bells, it had ended with the mob tearing the defenseless girl to pieces. Not only Babette was lost forever on the other side of a door, says Lucio. He points to the door that leads to the cockroach hell and explains its purpose to the woman. Let me throw in a book, says the woman. Lucio takes a blade from his desk drawer, goes to the cartons, and cuts some metal bands and tapes. She takes out a book, looks at the cover, reads the flaps, lingers over the author's portrait. Don't know him, she says. She pulls out another novel: *The Son of the Chief*. This one is marvelous, have you read it? Lucio shakes his head. She is not familiar with the third one, either. Not until the fourth is she able to say, This one should be cast straight into darkness, *Our Lady of the Circus*, a melodrama about dwarves and bearded women. Is there any ritual to be observed or do you just throw them through the opening? I just throw them. She goes toward the door and makes a throwing motion; turning to Lucio and seeing him with an impatient expression and his arms crossed, she drops it in. All right, she says, but this door ought to have a sign on it, something to indicate the fate of whoever passes through it. I don't know, says Lucio, going to the street door on hearing the rumbling of a heavy vehicle with a screechy suspension. The only one to see the sign would be me, and I don't need it. The air brakes hiss through all Icamole with greater authority than Melquisedec's goat bell. From the threshold of his library Lucio admires the water truck: government of the state, caution, capacity 35,000 liters. More water than in a month of round trips by wagon, old man, and mules.

The people line up with their receptacles, but the operator of the apparatus, without a by-your-leave, turns the hose on them, wetting all those standing around. Nobody complains, neither the old ladies whose scaly breasts are exposed, nor women having their period. From time to time the operator, fancying himself a cloud, shoots a spray upward that falls in a cool, fine drizzle, and from time to time, fancying himself a South American dictator, directs a strong stream at children, adults, and Josefina, the pregnant woman of Icamole. At other moments he remembers why the truck is there and fills a bucket at random, but those are few, for the people immediately start to boo and yell for him to shoot the water at them, hit me in the mouth, in the belly, in the behind, let it run, let it pour, let the earth soak it up, waste it, no matter, water is also for playing with, for dreaming, for shouting, for feeling its fondling. Go ahead, let the water run and make mud, which we haven't put our feet into for such a long time. Idiots, says Lucio, they pray to God and it's the devil who listens to them. It doesn't rain but the water truck comes around to stain our seabed. This Sunday must have been very productive in Villa de García. Whom did they beg? Or did the buses go on to Monterrey with them? Have pity, Señor Governor, we're thirsty, our children are getting dehydrated, the goats are dropping dead, old folks can't sweat anymore.

The woman goes over to Lucio. You don't look very happy, she says. He sits down on the floor and scrubs his hands over the sand. Everybody looks for a happy ending, he says, his face beaming, to break with natural destiny, to avoid tragedy; they pursue the banal and insipid, the frothy and womanly: they refuse to make literature.

Why that name? Remigio wonders as he looks at a photograph of Melquisedec on a wooden pony in the park, his mother standing alongside. There are eleven more photographs of men and women in the envelope that mean nothing to Remigio; aunts, perhaps, distant relatives, his father or grandfather. It is of no consequence, because they are images without a history. However, Melquisedec had told him about that afternoon in the park and, though in few words, enough for Remigio to imagine how she had directed him endearingly to look at the camera, which the boy had just done, and to smile, which he did not. The mother is beautiful, as Melquisedec had said, and she can readily be imagined as having a soft voice, perhaps a bit louder when she laughed, incapable of calling her son Melquisedec; no, she must have said to her husband, timidly, better Juan, Carlos, Octavio, although, then, her head bowed in obedience, after the slap in the face, she would have said, Yes, very well, his name shall be as you say. That's the reason for trying to get him to smile. Come now, dear, look at the camera and smile and remember that one day we were together and tried to make time stand still. The mother would eventually have died, no doubt of that, but why did that boy's fate have to be reflected in his face? Supposedly, one goes to the park to eat cotton candy, to burst a balloon, to dip one's hands in the fountain, to chase a ball or a dog, not to think: My mother is going to die, I am going to die, all of us are going to die. Even the wooden pony looks happier. Babette, just pulled out of the well, didn't appear that glum. Surely, it must be that having such an old man's name is hard on a little boy. He observes the tall trees with dense foliage in the background, so deeply green, no doubt, that the sepia tone of the image is turned copper-colored like the sand of the Icamole desert. That's how a photograph must look of Melquisedec in his cell, in his green undershorts, which are sepia like the rest of his body, sprawled out on a cot without sheets, between walls scrawled over with signatures and verses by drunks, thieves, and hoodlums. Because at this stage, there is no longer any doubt in Remigio's mind: Melquisedec had nothing to do with the business of Babette; if otherwise, they would have already made him talk about the well at Remigio's house, the librarian's son who has an avocado tree that grows the smoothest avocados in the whole country, which you can eat skin and all like a peach; no, much smoother than a peach, with salt or without, in a taco or without tortilla; delicate, delicious avocados, not like the kind with a snakeskin that they grow in other parts. Talk to Remigio, just ask him for avocados; don't leave Icamole without tasting them. Behind the trees in the photograph stands an old building, its heavily barred doorway protected by two guards. In the background a man wearing a jacket and hat. Many years have gone by; that man and the guards, too, must be dead. The wooden pony couldn't go anywhere; the boy would leave his childhood and the city to go to the desert. Remigio replaces the photograph in the envelope. Why Melquisedec? Icamole is a place people go away from, not to. Why would somebody who had been in a park come to a place like this, where there are no balloons or cotton candy? A week earlier it wouldn't have

bothered him if Melquisedec had suffered any kind of mishap.
Now, however, they have something in common, they are linked by
Babette's death, even though in a different way; but much as he
feels sorry for him, Remigio is not disposed to trade his luck for the
old man's.

The old guy didn't make it easy for us, says one of the cops.
Don't waste any more time, the lieutenant orders; the state police
got their hands on another suspect and figure to beat us out. They
open the door to the cell, and Melquisedec looks at them with that
same expression as when he was sitting on the wooden pony looking at the photographer.

Lucio is hungry. He has had nothing to eat but tortillas since Remigio came on like Kartukov to take back the basket of avocados. He envies cockroaches their ability to consume paper, stitching, and binder's glue, and to digest just as easily paperbacks, hardcovers, flaps, spines, poetry, and prose. When all is said and done, I did not go back on Herlinda's plan, Lucio reassures himself; I converted the lower floor into the storeroom for balanced feeds. He goes out and follows the scent of cooking in the street as far as Señora Robles's window. He stays there for a moment, seduced no longer by the aroma but by the vision of a bounteous kitchen with fruits, vegetables, and, lying on a table, feet up, a luscious hen that did not die before having produced her quota of eggs. That kitchen does not match the view from Haslinger's Peak of Icamole, a town on the verge of condemning everybody to starvation. Lucio moves over to the open door, from where he can see the five members of the family seated around the table; he is unable to make out what they are eating, but the glasses are brimming with lemonade. The family recognizes him, and Señor Robles invites him in. How about a taco? Lucio remains mute for a moment. He is hungry enough to eat Herlinda's salty soup. I just stopped by to tell your children that I have some adventure books; maybe they would be interested to know that the Amarids are attacking the kingdom of Toranio. He leaves immediately and goes to a hill behind the chapel where a healthy, still juicy, nopal stands. He takes out his knife and cuts off two paddles. He prides himself on his ability to obtain food from nature even though nature has been so mean in these parts. When he visited Monterrey during the statewide librarians' convention, his colleagues made him feel awkward, out of place, because he was fearful about crossing streets with traffic, because he tripped on the city hall escalators and covered his ears when a car back-fired. At the working sessions, discussions were held on indexing systems, book-preservation methods, lending supervision, and how to build readership. At the end, there was a meeting in which the librarians discussed their needs, and such subjects were taken up as salaries, air conditioning, weatherproofing, restroom facilities, and lighting. Lucio offered the suggestion that a letter be sent to French translators requesting that they translate the word *rue*. The idea was met with a prolonged silence, all pens apparently busily engaged. In the course of the convention only one other librarian sought him out for a chat. It was on the last night before he was to return to Icamole. After several beers, Lucio felt sufficiently confi-dent to express his preferences in books. The other man listened without comment, drinking and popping salted peanuts into his mouth. Around midnight, he picked a bit of shell from between his teeth and with an air of superiority passed judgment. You have the three prejudices of the small-towner: against Spaniards, against gringos, and against women. He took another swallow of beer and went on. In the city, we have overcome the first two. Lucio dropped a bill on the table and left. He swore never to attend another of those meetings or to set foot in Monterrey or any other city. Lost in thought, he pricked his thumb on a cactus thorn. As he sucked away the drop of blood, he said to himself that he would love to abandon all those librarians in the middle of the desert; let's see how long they survive, what good to them is their ability to cross streets, to keep their balance on an escalator, and to tolerate backfiring cars. Their intelligence, then, would be useless, would turn into ignorance, and my ingenuity would become erudition. Lucio, please tell us which plants are edible, how we can get water, how to ride a mule, how to sleep at night amid snakes and coyotes; they would lose dignity before Señor Robles: Yes, please, for pity's sake let me have a taco. In Icamole Lucio trusts his brain to the point that he has rejected everything taught him in Monterrey. Lending control? I don't lend anything. Conservation? My books have to last only a short time; when I die they can shrivel up and expire, too. And, more than anything else, he had scorn for cataloguing systems. A specialist explained how to classify books according to subject, date of publication, nationality of author, and other variables, by assigning numbers and letters. He never spoke of separating good and bad books, but, rather, insisted that the main classification be based on the concept of fiction and nonfiction. Lucio was utterly disillusioned on hearing the pronouncements of that specialist. He was unable to accept that book people, people of letters, could have made that classification; it was impossible that they would be so lacking in words as to call something by a name that it is not. Furthermore, where is the borderline between one and the other? Into which do memoirs of a president fall? A historical novel? Lives of the saints? On which side would *A Soldier's Testimony* go? If there are contradictions between two history books or two holy books, who decides which gets to be called fiction? Lucio closed his notebook and no longer listened to that faker. His ideas were clear. A history book talks of things that happened while a novel talks of things that happen, and so historical time contrasts with that of the novel, which Lucio calls the permanent present, an immediate time, tangible and real. Babette exists in that time, is more real than a national hero buried in the rotunda of eminent persons; Babette could never be in a section marked fiction; in that permanent present, a mysterious hand seizes Babette again and again each time the book is opened to the last page, and the girl irrevocably throws her umbrella into the Seine in Chapter 12; Babette is not nor will be turned into dust.

Back home, he fills a pot with water, throws in the two nopal paddles without stripping off the thorns. In order to avoid heating up the room, he goes down the stairway, builds a small fire outdoors at one side of the library, and sets his food on it to cook. There he can imagine that the aroma from some other house is the one rising from his pot.

Lucio points to the left to indicate where Porfirio Díaz's army entered, and to his right, where the *federales* came from. This soil has a history and prehistory, he said, because an ichthyosaur also came from over there to eat a fish, and why not? That was the route Melquisedec, carrying Babette, would have had to take, just where the current is strongest and twists the seaweed and hones the reefs. The woman nods. Now she is dressed in white, and from a distance it is impossible to tell where her sleeve ends and her arm begins. But the people don't know anything about this, Lucio goes on. When they find saurian teeth, an embedded trilobite, cartridges from that battle, they put them into a plastic bag and take them to sell on the side of the highway. With respect to prehistory, if anybody asks, all they do is shrug: I don't know, Señor, they are animals from long ago. But when it has to do with history, they behave differently. They have made changes in it so as to raise the price of cartridges. These are Pancho Villa's bullets, they say, because Porfirio Díaz isn't worth as much in the Mexican imagination. And they have ended up believing it themselves: the battle of 1876 is expunged, and they believe blindly in another one that would have had to have taken place forty years later, because it is unjust to say that Pancho Villa roamed all over the North, his army raping and impregnating women on the plains, in the woods, and on the mountains, and that the women of Icamole were left unmolested. We want sons of Pancho Villa, too, they will have yelled. Here we are, our legs spread, and with cowards for husbands; come galloping in on your horse, shooting into the air, shooting to kill; we want sons with your eyes, your belly, your guts, and balls like yours, not like that Wailer of Icamole, the perfect army officer, the perfect gentleman, the perfect president, top hat, spats, and all. And, fortunately, that Pedro Montes neglected to date his letter to Evangelina, and though he spoke of a battle in the month of May, he did not mention the year, the sides, names, or causes, so it is easier to worship him in the belief that he died forty years later. Long live Pancho Villa, you sonsofbitches, and the Virgin of Guadalupe. They worship both, create their own novels. They believe in them the way you and I believe in Babette. They also believe in the yarns about Evangelina's letter, in the *Guadalupe Hymnal* even though they haven't seen anything but the cover, believe in the novels of the Bible, the resurrection, angels, ships with animals of all the earth, in hell and paradise, the sun that stood still, snakes that talk and pigs that leap into a ravine, angels, demons, the crucified, and so many things that nobody has ever seen and never will except in the form of words. And so I cannot understand the resistance to using my library, why they think there is a gap between life and paper.

Holding his hand, the woman feels the rough, desert-skin texture unlike that of a city person's. However, the touch he feels is very like Herlinda's. If not for the age difference, she says, I would have fallen in love with you by now. He lowers his eyes and for a moment forgets about living at the bottom of the sea. Is the woman serious? Or just quoting Masumi so as to get me to reply like Yoshikazu? Lucio elects to keep quiet. Although Yoshikazu is an old man, he has won certain privileges after having dispatched so many enemies with his katana; privileges I have not earned by caring for the books in my library. The woman takes leave by bowing her head and returns to her car. You don't have to love me, says Lucio when he knows she is out of earshot. Suffice it that you serve me. And he waves his katana in the air to frighten off Emperor Eichiro's men.

The water truck comes to Icamole for the second time. Now there is no playing with the water, no wetting people down; the vehicle is the same, but it has a different driver. From the window of the cab the man asks the first person he comes to, How many families are you? Señora Urdaneta shrugs. Not very many, she answers, and he explains to her that his instructions are to stop at each house and deliver all the water that can be stored; he will also fill animal troughs and pour water into septic tanks for anybody who wishes. Word gets around, and by the time the truck has stopped by all the houses, the consensus is that the driver is businesslike but friendly, careful to turn the hose off in time to avoid wasting water; however, the people prefer the previous operator, because when men, women, children ended up all soaked, they felt as though the water was not from a truck provided by the government but rain sent by Providence.

Although annoyed by the visit of the huge truck and its rumbling, Lucio takes advantage of his turn to fill a tank. He wants to take a bath, shave, wash his clothes and sheets. The way Babette's mother avoided being close to him did not pass unnoticed. Yes, books do narrow the gap between us, but other factors widen it; a bath could help reduce the gap. We would be able to sit together and read *Rebecca in the Afternoons*, the book half on her lap, half on mine. Lucio directs the truck to the tank in back of the library. Fill it up, he says; a person has to wash himself once in a while. The driver makes no comment, shuts the water off when finished, and begins to roll up the hose. Any news? asks Lucio. Getting no answer after a few moments, he asks again, Will you keep coming around? The man nods. I'll be back as long as it doesn't rain, he says, gets into the truck, and moves on to the next house. Lucio wets his face and neck and goes into the library. He wants a good book for the afternoon, preferably one about a traveler and his adventures or a youngster who wants to be a soccer player, one of those novels in which death is a remote element. He picks a book at random out of the box he had opened for the woman: *Bitterness*. The picture on the cover of a girl carrying books and a tennis racquet against a campus background is enough for him to imagine the contents. Another of those, he says to himself, by the kind of writer who ends up teaching in some gringo university and then goes in for novelizing his affair with a student. Could his story be different? Maybe in that the girl's name is Evelyn and he is a professor of sociology instead of literature. Of course, this is a man who has led an orderly life until Evelyn, in a short skirt, comes into his office for a consultation. From that moment on there will be a mixture of guilt and frenzy, long paragraphs in the first person to justify the professor and thereby oblige the reader to empathize with him. Yes, she's nineteen and he's over fifty, she with the world before her, he with a family to support, but being a decent man, he truly loves her, and nobody has a right to interfere in his private life or to question his professional integrity. For that reason, it is unfair that he be treated like a criminal, as though it were not obvious that he is the victim, because sooner or later, at her parents' insistence, Evelyn will end up leaving him, and he will realize that he ruined his marriage and his career in exchange for a memory in his old age. He is about to cast the book into hell when it occurs to him to read the back cover; perhaps there will be an original twist; perhaps if the author were teaching in a Latin American university, then if he wished to gambol with any one of his students, there would be no moral or professional onus. Such is not the case; the comments of the editor concern the social pressures imposed upon love, how even the closest of friends will constitute an inquisition in view of the disruption of an ordinary way of life. Your Grace, says Lucio aloud, what should be the fate of this book? To the stake with it is the verdict, and so he acts, seventy thousand words condemned on the spot.

He tries a second book: Igor Pankin, *The Blue Snows*. There is no indication of the nature of the contents. The cover shows a wooded, snow-covered landscape; the commentary on the back cover speaks of prose of austere beauty, of an author whose work is presumed to represent an original approach to the possibilities of the novel form. Lucio decides to read the concluding paragraph because he knows that a good ending is an indication of a good novel. The same is not true of openings. Bronislava's hand stretches out through the train window to caress Radoslav's face. You know that as soon as I reach Kaliningrad, I will be a married woman and go by another name. She regrets having spoken. Words are superfluous. If that final moment is to be remembered by them, most precious is the silence, the determination not to cry. The train begins to move. Radoslav paces next to it, lengthening his stride as it gathers speed. Wait, he suddenly yells, I'm forgetting something. He unbuttons his overcoat, rummages in the pockets to come out with a box wrapped in brown paper, a procedure which slows him down so that Bronislava's train gains several meters on him. She watches him run, holding out the box and shouting at people in his way as he races ahead. When the train is about to open a gap impossible for human legs to breach, Radoslav flings the box at the window. It strikes her outstretched palm, but she cannot make the catch, and it falls toward the tracks. It is not essential for her to have it, to open it. She knows what it contains, knows perfectly well. She collapses into her seat and, yes, now begins to cry, because she will have no keepsake worthy of Radoslav to take away with her; what her memory will bring back to her will be the image of a man running awkwardly through the station, shouting, throwing a box as wasted as the remainder of their lives.

The want of a worthy keepsake, Lucio says to himself, just as in my case. Bronislava sees her man running after a train, and I see Herlinda before a bowl of salty vegetable soup. Lucio's intuition tells him that *The Blue Snows* will find a place on a shelf of his favorite books, since he is intrigued as well by the contents of the little box in brown paper and now believes the comment on the back cover inasmuch as he does encounter prose of austere beauty without superfluous verbiage or dramatic effects in that concluding paragraph. Another novelist would have made sure that the box had fallen onto the tracks and described the iron wheels crushing, disintegrating it, turning Bronislava's illusions into an emptiness; would have transformed the final sob into a torrent of words plus tears, eyes, grief, wet cheeks, handkerchiefs, sobs, and sighs, and a final call to the reader to pity that woman, saying that the train was lost in the distance, leaving in sight only steam, which vanished like Radoslav's hopes, forever. Fortunately, there was none of that; I read only the last paragraph and feel that I know Bronislava, that nothing in the world would please me more than to be traveling in that car, in the seat alongside hers, to offer her my embrace: Come Bronislava, come with me, I will comfort you from here to Kaliningrad, and I will remain beside you and will love you just as Radoslav loves you. An ending with a train drawing away in the distance is not original, Lucio says to himself, but Pankin is justified, his restraint gives him the right to that and more, even to not revealing the contents of the box.

He puts *The Blue Snows* on his desk and sets about reading it when he is struck by an idea. The uncle gives Babette an umbrella; the box thrown by Radoslav must contain a gift, some object of importance to each of them in their relationship. I must give Babette's mother a present of some kind, since it is obvious that sooner or later she will be suspending her visits to Icamole, will go off in her car like Bronislava on the train, and I will have nothing to throw to her, to put into her hands. A book? No. She is perfectly familiar with *The Death of Babette*, the one novel that would have intimate significance. Nor can I give her a fossil, as beautifully graven as it may be, since in Icamole it is no different from any stone. It is not easy for him to find an answer; he knows that a city woman would not welcome what here in the country is considered a gift: a chicken, a goat, a snakeskin.

He hears the truck motor and puts off reading and consideration of his gift problem for later. He runs out to the street and motions to the driver to stop. He starts talking the moment he has climbed on the running board. They threw him out of a pickup truck moving at full speed on the highway, didn't they? The driver shuts off the motor to make sure he is hearing right. Lucio thinks that this is exactly the scene in which a second-rate writer has the driver asking: What are you talking about? I'm talking about Melquisedec, about how they killed him, he answers. He's not dead, says the man, he's in jail now, and for the rest of his life. He already confessed to kidnapping the youngster, and now the people in Villa de García are gossiping about all he did to the poor child, a lovely little girl, I know, because the police showed me her photograph, very beautiful, and that's why any man would like to kidnap her. But it's not right, no, Señor; had a boy done it, you could understand, but an old man like Melquisedec; that guy had no right even to think about her. He's alive, the man repeats, but the sooner he dies, the better.

Lucio returns to his desk and remains gazing at *The Blue Snows* for several minutes, then he starts to turn pages and discovers the translator's notes. In one of them he explains that *babushka* means grandmother; in another, that *galuschki* is a Ukrainian dish, but does not mention its ingredients or how it is prepared; and in still another, explains that the Russian letter Z has the same phonetic value as in French, a piece of information that angers Lucio. The flap indicates that Pankin was born in Kirov and died in exile in Paris, having spent time in Siberia. He has no confidence in this last item; he supposes that not all writers who claim to have been prisoners have actually been in prison. He shuts the book and realizes that his mind is not on the printed words but on the truck driver's, and ends up admitting that he doesn't feel like reading that afternoon.

They go into the chapel, and Lucio shows her the peaches-in-syrup jar with Evangelina's letter inside. This is an original, he says, and the difference from a painting by an artist is that in literature it is permissible to touch up originals, cross out, inform an author you forgot an accent here, you have extra words there, you got a date wrong or a fact, to ask him, Must you say a heavy downpour when a downpour is heavy without the adjective? But I didn't bring you here to talk about that, but to tell you that right under this altar lie the remains of Pedro Montes, a soldier who fought in Porfirio Díaz's army. You're not going to tell me about that battle all over again, are you? interrupts the woman. I am going to but in different way, because the line that stretches from that event ends up tying in with your daughter, with Babette. Let us for a moment imagine Don Porfirio here in these parts, on his horse, a stalwart figure on the battlefield, shouting commands to his troops, ready to fight sword to sword, rifle to rifle, seeing his men fall at his side, nevertheless presenting to the enemy the proud image of a forty-five-year-old warrior, an age at which city gentlemen, having no army at their command, will yell at a waitress slow in bringing the check, and none such as those would be capable of staying the course, of crying out orders and setting an example as the bullets whistle by. And such an example of valor, comparable only to that of

Yoshikazu, gave him the right to be president of his country for many years. But Mexico is unwilling to accept great men if they happen to be Mexican. And so the day came when an insignificant fellow threatened to begin killing people if he did not get out of the country, and Don Porfirio, weary of bloodshed, boarded a ship that weighed anchor in Veracruz, there no longer being a sea in Icamole. Let us now imagine this Don Porfirio exiled in Paris, yearning for his homeland at an age when practically everybody is dead; imagine him taking a stroll on the same streets that Babette knew, erect with his walking stick, crossing the bridge over the Seine where the umbrella fell in. Undoubtedly, and perhaps without being aware of it, he will have passed by the very doorway in which the girl was swallowed up, even could have heard the bell still there after so many years to announce callers. While regarding from his window the Eiffel Tower, which Babette was never able to see, Don Porfirio received news that the little man who drove him out of the country, that Francisco Madero, who tried to play at being president, had died like a wimp, in tears, on the run, begging for mercy, fleeing bullets a few of which inevitably went through his back in a death acceptable not even to Melquisedec. Mexico had exiled the best of Mexicans in exchange for which it became the booty of vultures. That's why the Wailer of Icamole became the Wailer of Paris when he finally realized on the second of July of 1915 that he would never be going back to his native land, on the brink of extinction. He died shortly before another celebration of the French Revolution, before another anniversary of the death of Babette; and then, not even dead, harmless, silent, incapable of brandishing a weapon, was he permitted to return to his country. His bones, therefore, are now in the Montparnasse cemetery, very near the remains of Pierre Laffitte.

Lucio walks to the other end of the chapel and remains facing the wall for a moment or two, then makes a half-turn and with his hand outstretched goes toward the woman. It is an honor to meet such a distinguished man, soldier, and president. She hesitates before shaking his hand. Pierre Laffitte, at your service, he says. Porfirio Díaz, she says, likewise at your service. I know you very well, says Laffitte; all Frenchman know and respect you and even fear you. It was you who defeated us on the fifth of May; we know that it was Zaragoza who gave the commands, but you were the one who carried them out and who swamped us with your cavalry charges, riddled us with bullets, forced us to retreat; you were the victor in that battle won not under Zaragoza's command but with your balls and your men. That is why Zaragoza was to die in a hut like a mangy dog while you passed away in a mansion in Paris surrounded by your family, the highest dignitaries, and, by order of the president of the Republic of France, with Napoleon's sword in your hands. If your devotion to me is so great, Don Porfirio says, I must ask a favor of you. Pierre Laffitte nods: Anything you want of me except that I betray my homeland. Have no concern, my request is a simpler one: just tell me where Babette is. I lost her on the other side of a door and know nothing more of her; whether she is dead or alive doesn't matter to me, but just as you and I have the certainty of finding ourselves in Montparnasse, I must have that certainty about Babette. Laffitte settles down in a chair. He chooses to fix his gaze on the floor as he speaks: I am sorry, but my homeland is the novel; I cannot become a squealer like Zimbrowski's father. Don Porfirio goes over to him and slaps him in the face. As the only Indian who truly became a Parisian, I order you to tell me where the hell Babette is or Babette's body or Babette's bones, or her dust or her spirit, or her name, or her nothingness.

Without raising his eyes from the floor, Pierre Laffitte gets up and goes to the chapel door. From there he lets his gaze stray over Icamole in admiration of its hills and mountains and cactuses. Come, Don Porfirio, he says, and waits in silence until he has him at his side. You must know how many men fell in the Battle of Icamole, how many lie buried on this sea bottom. Examining it closely, it looks lovelier than Montparnasse; the waves more beautiful than its litanies, the corals, than its headstones, the cactuses, than its crosses; besides, there are young people here who died by violence, not old, ailing ones like you and me, whose bones are already turning to dust; and here is the Babette of yours, of mine, of all the women who have lost a daughter; there she is, beneath that avocado tree you can see on the right, the only green tree we have left. The entire sea has been flooded by desert, but Babette's island remains.

Rest in peace, says Don Porfirio. Rest in peace, repeats Laffitte.

Three women come into the library. We think it was you who marked up Evangelina's letter, one of them says. We had it looked up in teacher Rocha's dictionary and yes it is true that you have to write faithful with only one l, but nobody has a right to change a sacred document. Another of the women, a Bible in her hand, goes over to Lucio. Laying it on his desk opened to a page toward the end she points out a pair of verses that have been underlined. Read this. He turns the Bible to see the lines and, as he used to do when he had people around, he reads aloud: For I testify unto every man that heareth the words of the prophecy of this book, If any man shall add unto these things, God shall add unto him the plagues that are written in this book. And if any man shall take away from the words of the book of this prophecy, God shall take away his part of the tree of life, and of the holy city, and the things which are written in this book. The wording seems clumsy to him, with unnecessary repetitions; he rereads silently and only then raises his eyes. The third woman speaks to him of risking his soul with these goings-on about changing sacred words, but Lucio is no longer listening, his mind concentrating on the passage in the Bible. Why that warning? Why this message that no writer would dare address to an editor? Not even a poet with an ego swollen by a Pavlov Prize. A comma, an accent, and I will do you in, will kick you out of the city. Quite a guy the author of the Bible, he says to himself. Muttering, the women leave. Lucio remains absorbed momentarily in the verses, going back a page to read the beginning of the chapter. And he shewed me a pure river of the water of life, clear as crystal. Clear as crystal? Lucio questions that. I know of no more hackneyed simile, unless, perhaps, some by those Nordic writers who speak of faces white as snow without consideration of desert people who have never seen snow. He turns back in the book to the first chapter of Genesis. In the beginning God created the heavens and the earth. He shakes his head. Why clarify that the beginning is the beginning? He strikes out the first words and reads aloud: God created the heavens and the earth. Much better, he says to himself. He skips pages and continues reading. By your great power they shall be still as stones. Lucio has always distrusted similes. Still as stones, he repeats in a whisper, by the same token, they could also be still as stumps or shoes or anything at all that comes to mind. After reconsidering his opinion he ends up accepting the simile, since it goes unnoticed in its very ordinariness; to have written they shall be as still as fingernails would provoke the reader into considering it outlandish and distract his attention from the text. Anyway, the best correction seems to him simply to say, By your great power, Lord, they shall be still. Despite his distrust of similes, Lucio almost never consigns a book to hell for being hackneyed, no matter how extreme, not even when, instead of guiding the reader, it disorients him. He felt as though the world were crashing down around him, like the last man on earth, unimaginable thoughts for Lucio to be having, foolish but tolerable words. But he would deliver a novel at once to the cockroaches, no matter how attractive it seemed to him, if the author resorted to the cinema to make his point clear. Two weeks ago he had withdrawn a novel for that very reason: Taking her by the hand, James smiled at her like Peter O'Donohue in *Valley of the Seagulls*, which Mary Anne had seen at least ten times on the big screen at the theater on Eighth Street. How am I possibly going to imagine that smile? exclaimed Lucio, who hadn't set foot in a movie theater in years. He got rid of the book without a second thought, despite knowing that the O'Donohue smile was James's first step in seducing Mary Anne. He looks down on motion pictures, but his aversion for those authors is based on something else. They do not deserve to be called writers, he believes, if, instead of taking the trouble to describe a smile, a hairstyle, a glance, an attitude, they would rather send me to watch a film. He closes the Bible, resting it on its spine and letting it fall open to any page. There he begins to read: And thou shalt eat the fruit of thine own body, the flesh of thy sons and of thy daughters, which the Lord thy God hath given thee, in the siege, and in the straitness, wherewith thine enemies shall distress thee. This is, indeed, very good, he nods in satisfaction. He does repeat the word *flesh* three times, but that doesn't matter; rather, it lends intensity and rhythm. As for the Gospels, it is clear that writer and editor should have chosen the best of the four, the most complete or poetic or revelatory or, as they usually do, the most commercial, and suppress the other three. He decides to read only the verse in each of them in which Christ dies. They are easy to find, since in that edition of the Bible, the words appear in red each time the Savior speaks. Matthew says, Jesus, when he had cried again with a loud voice, yielded up the ghost. Mark redacts more concisely: And Jesus cried with a loud voice, and gave up the ghost. Both describe a loud voice, and to Lucio that seems good, since to use shout or scream as synonyms would detract from the dignity of the final moment. Luke says practically the same thing, only clarifying what Jesus cried out in a loud voice: Father, into thy hands I commend my spirit. A good statement for dying, but they seem to Lucio like words to be said in a whisper; difficult to imagine them exclaimed in a loud voice. Finally, he reads John: When Jesus therefore had received the vinegar, he said, It is finished. And he bowed his head, and gave up the ghost. He studied it again and concluded that John was the best. According to John, Christ said, did not shout; according to John, he realized it was all over; according to John, he bowed his head. It is finished turned out to be a more powerful phrase than Father, into thy hands I commend my spirit. It was restrained, definitive, summing up acceptance of finality. Although, without doubt, as an evangelist, Pierre Laffitte would have been more concise, more forceful, would have obviated the need to say that He gave up the ghost or to make any direct reference to death. Laffitte's version would simply indicate: It is finished, said Jesus when he had received the vinegar and bowed his head.

This is not the first time Lucio has held a Bible in his hands. He has read it before and considers it an excellent book, if only a better job of editing had been done, if only it didn't display the excesses of the novelist who is paid by the word. He closes the volume and goes to the bookshelves to find a place for it. A good book, he says, but with defects. He decides not to put it with his favorites, not among *The Song of the Forgotten One*, *The Pond*, *Treachery*, *The Gypsy Woman and the Blind Man*, *Two Grams of Innocence*, *The Death of Babette*, and so many others. Forgive me, he says, but you are far from perfect, at least as a writer. Right here, on these shelves, I have examples by many authors who have done better than you.

He notices that it is getting dark in his library. A passing cloud, no doubt. Lucio settles the Bible in between *Nostalgia for Your Image* and *Battles in the Night* and goes out to the street. It is no ordinary cloud, not white as a face white as snow.

It is raining with such a vengeance that ditches and streams overflow, causing a flood to pour through the streets. Lucio takes off his shoes and sits on the library steps watching beads of round goat shit race by floating in barnyard swill like cereal pellets in milk. The people come out to get soaked and for a repetition of the hullabaloo of the water truck's first visit, except that now they don't have to take turns. The rain falls and water runs equally for all. Señora Urdaneta sits down in the middle of the street, legs spread against the current; a pair of naked kids leap about; several women go off to the chapel to make sure the downpour is not getting into the building; Fatso Antúnez lies down, rolling his body from side to side, screaming, Help, the current is carrying me away. This rain is different from the rain in Madrid, Lucio thinks, imagining pavement in place of mud and girls in short skirts leaping over puddles and visualizing the newly arrived African immigrant wet to the skin, and the waiter busily sweeping the floor because the customers are leaving footprints. I should have given *Autumn in Madrid* another chance, if only for another ten pages; maybe the lover was about to finish his letter, and the author would have let up on the syrupy language and gotten back to text concerning the pig in the hands of the slaughterers and would have ended up killing off the immigrant like a pig, despite MacAllister's preaching that color plays no role, and if, in the end, there should be a little boy asking his grandmother why such things go on, she would have no hesitation in replying: Because we people are black, and that, my boy, is why they keep busting our balls.

However, *Autumn in Madrid* has been withdrawn, and there's no turning those pages back.

Lucio spits into the water, wishing the torrent would carry the gob straight into Fatso Antúnez's face. He says to himself that there are also novels about obese idiot boys who murder little girls, mounting them, sweating, unsure of what to do right then. One such is Bobby Masterson, the retarded character in *Life in the Potato Fields*. On a farm in Ireland he has for weeks been peeping through the window at his cousin Lucille, a wisp of a cousin, the farm right on the coast. It doesn't matter whether the blind is up or down; it is all the same to Bobby if he is seeing or imagining Lucille's movements from the moment she enters her bedroom until she falls sleep on a bed with squeaky springs. On St. Patrick's Day eve, all the adults are in the nearby town, and what follows is so predictable that Lucio says to himself that the boy is going to kill her, no doubt about it, but hopefully he will do it right there in the bed; hopefully he won't take her to the stable. But he does, and he throws her onto the straw to the bleating of some sheep. Bobby does not know what to do, so he gets on top of her with all his clothes on and without trying to undress her. The sweat runs down his face to the end of his nose, which becomes a funnel from which the drops fall into his cousin's eyes, who can no longer tell the difference between the other's sweat and her own tears. Bobby decides to kill her, the writer does not explain why, only mentioning an inner voice that says, Kill her, kill her. And to do so he topples his entire weight on top of her, smothering her little by little, telling her all the while that he loves her and asking her if she loves him. Lucio needed no explanations: Bobby has to kill his cousin because he is a fat idiot, and fat idiots do not appear in stories to steal potatoes or to shear sheep; fat idiots provoke disaster and die tragically in the penultimate chapter. Bobby would have to fall off a cliff into the sea without anybody's ever learning what became of him; Lucio finishes the novel, grateful that the stable was never burned down.

Fatso Antúnez carries on his rolling and yelling. Help, somebody take pity on me. Lucio reinforces his idea of barnyard swill and goes over to the Icamole Bobby Masterson. Get up, you fat slob, he fetches him a kick with his bare foot, you don't do that to a little girl, much less if it isn't even to enjoy her. You should have been in Melquisedec's place; the police would have loved torturing all that fat and those woman's nipples of yours. You'd have good reason to holler for help, screaming because of the knitting needles in your ass. Another kick. The fat boy keeps lying there but without rolling, looking at Lucio in terror. The stream is carrying less and less excrement. Throwing Melquisedec from a speeding pickup truck wouldn't be the same as throwing you. You'd be a sight to remember, unbelievable, a huge pustule burst open on a roadside. He gives him another kick, and the fat boy whimpers. Señora Urdaneta, closing her legs and standing up, yells, Don't hurt the boy.

The torrent swells, having swept away one of Lucio's shoes. He knows that there is still time to find it, but does not want those people to see him running after something dark-colored that could be his shoe or a dead rat.

Remigio had told him that Babette was also missing a shoe; perhaps the torrent would carry both away to the same place.

He goes, dripping, into his library, itching to punch somebody in the nose. He watches through the window at the people of Icamole soaking in the rain. European writers associate a gray sky with sadness, no doubt, Lucio thinks, never having seen it rain in Icamole. Only Babette is different; she gets wet and smiles, thinking of the raindrops on the roof as musical beats. But the Seine is not the same as this rivulet of manure. Babette, without an umbrella, and Señora Urdaneta, with her legs spread, are not the same.

Señor Laffitte, I lost many men on this soil, says Don Porfirio, but not one, not all of them together, is worth a hair on Babette's head or, when you write about Babette, just the word *hair*, if you prefer. Perhaps a wife or a mother or even a father would mourn them, or they themselves would, if death throes gave them the time, if the bullet or shell didn't immediately blow out their brains. Perhaps the Wailer of Icamole mourned them, but from then on they no longer mattered except as food for flies and worms: unless it was Pedro Montes who, like you, matters only for what he wrote. Babette is and always will be; my soldiers were, and that is all. I was. That is why men like me must succeed in making history into literature. Ask people, ask even those who have devoted themselves to studying me. People will say, Oh, yes, Don Porfirio, and come up with vague notions: a dictator who was reelected many times, went to Paris, died there, possibly a good soldier, from the South, from Oaxaca or Tabasco, I believe; it was his fault that the Revolution broke out. Some will argue that my government should be called a Porfiriate or Porfirianism, and almost everybody, on hearing my name, will picture a man of eighty, in semiprofile, a thick gray mustache, various decorations on his chest and an arrogant air about him, but nobody will recall such phrases as Porfirio awoke and, not feeling like getting up, pulled the covers over himself so his mother wouldn't see him; he licked his fingertips one by one before stroking Carmelita's tightened nipples; he kissed his son on the forehead and promised to teach him that very week to ride a horse; before leaving the hotel to board the *Ipiranga*, en route to exile, he looked at himself in the mirror to find there, for the first time, a weak man, in decline. Do you understand me, Señor Laffitte? Even though it be only a few lines, I need you to write about me; the end of Don Porfirio cannot be a doctor announcing that my faculties have ceased to function, or a casket being lowered into a Montparnasse grave; no, Señor Laffitte, dust I am, but I do not wish myself to be turned into dust but into language, into your language, in *The Death of Don Porfirio*, by Pierre Laffitte.

The conversation had been initiated in the library; now both are at Remigio's door. Is it here? the woman asks. Lucio raps with his knuckles. Open up, you have a visitor. She speaks firmly: Señor Laffitte, I am waiting for an answer. I can't say, Don Porfirio, it's years since I've written. She takes his hands, opting for a softer tone. Please, Monsieur Laffitte, she says, squeezing until he finally accedes.

Lucio stands in front of the avocado tree pointing toward its roots. Babette is here, he says; the rain has arrived, and, Icamole will soon be green again, but this tree never lost color or vitality. Babette is prose but at the same time, poetry, an idea for a dance that never took place, a lover who never appeared, an umbrella in Uncle André's memory, the mother who asks herself where she could be, the word *Babette* unchangeable though translated into twenty languages, though printed in roman, italic, or Celtic letters. But Babette is also three-fourths water, organic matter, intestine with feces halfway that are now fertilizer; Babette is, at the same time, nitrites and nitrates, saliva and sweat and tears and urine, is phosphorus and calcium and iron and potassium, is hair and mucus, is the last supper in her stomach. Babette is all these sprouting avocados peeping out among the leaves and branches, smooth avocados that will give up their seed to be planted one day in this orchard that will shelter all Babette's descendants. Lucio takes the woman by the hand and leads her to the foot of the tree. As Uncle André said, Look at your daughter and see the sun, look at your daughter and see the earth; the sun is of God, the earth is the homeland, and Babette belongs to both. The woman takes hold of the tree with her two hands, closes her eyes, and bows her head.

Remigio leads Lucio by the arm into the house. Why did you

bring that woman here? Don't worry, she will visit her daughter's grave and remain silent, with no desire to dig, seeking no vengeance or guilty parties beyond Melquisedec. Besides, not I, but Pierre Laffitte, told her, and the woman has no need to see the body; the words suffice. The conversation is interrupted when Lucio enters Remigio's bedroom and sees the empty basket and the bedsheets smeared with avocado. Had the avocados been red, it would have looked like the scene of a violent crime, but their deep-green color obviates such an allusion, as outlandish as a simile out of Soledad Artigas. Remigio points to Alberto Santín's book on a table next to the bed. That is the first novel I have ever read all the way through, he says. Santín doesn't know much; he is incapable of talking about a murder when it is obvious that he hasn't even wrung the neck of a chicken, wouldn't have the nerve to stick a pig. Being your first novel, you notice many things, Lucio observes. Did you read his biography on the flap? He is a city writer for city read-ers and one who sits on a porcelain crapper, knows nothing of latrines. But there is something he does understand very well, says Remigio; you refrained from getting rid of the book on account of a physical shortcoming of the character's. Yes, Lucio admits, that seemed original to me; it breaks with the habit of authors who put their ego above art. It seems to me your solidarity is more than lit-erary, Remigio eyes him defiantly. Lucio runs his fingers through his hair: It never mattered to your mother, and you are my son. Remigio duplicates the gesture of fingers through his hair. It doesn't matter to the avocados, either. Embarrassed, he bundles up the sheets and throws them on the floor. I suppose you love that woman. Lucio puts the book back on the table and plunges his hands into his pockets to keep them still. Yes, he says, the way old men love: with resignation. Calculating that the silence lends more clarity than words, Remigio elects to add nothing. Lucio picks up the conversation, saying, Yesterday I saw Señora Urdaneta under the rain. She was laughing; she is missing a couple of teeth at least, and her belly shook in all four folds. Then I turned to *The Death of Babette*, to read the passage about the spring storm. Babette lay down on the sidewalk looking up at the sky and discovered a new way of enjoying the rain; she blinked with each drop that fell into her eyes. Blinking was unavoidable, as was her bursting into laughter, and, once her mouth was open, the rain took over her five senses. People were running for shelter and had to step over the joyful girl, tumbled like a corpse but more alive than all those watching her. An old man decided to lie down next to her, their heads almost touching and legs at opposite poles. How old are you, little girl? Twelve. Well, if my arithmetic doesn't fail me, I would have done this sixty-two years ago, but at that time my mother would have scolded me; now it is my doctor who will. They both laughed when a woman passing nearby called them morons.

Icamole and Paris, says Remigio, what a difference. Lucio nods. Today I read that passage until I had it memorized, but it did me little good, because it isn't the girl lying in front of the Palace of the Tuileries who has been popping into my mind but Señora Urdaneta with her legs spread. Paris or Icamole, the differences never concerned me, but, in any case, Icamole comes out ahead. At least that's what I thought until the rains came. I wanted to see Babette and only Señora Urdaneta appears. That's why Babette's mother must stay in Icamole. My window isn't Don Porfirio's window; I can't see the Eiffel Tower from it, but I do want to have a glimpse, at least from time to time, of that woman weeping next to the avocado tree. Is that why you brought her? Remigio makes a sign to Lucio to follow him; in the kitchen he points to rolls on the table. Do you want to establish a link between that woman and the tree? Do you want her here for every anniversary? Every special occasion? Lucio picks up a roll and takes several bites before speaking. She says that age separates us; otherwise, she would love me. Remigio smiles. Did you believe her? It is starting to rain again, a drizzle that, nevertheless, makes itself heard on the metal roof. The woman remains beside the avocado tree without moving. They are not words to be believed in, Lucio replies; they are words that take root in my mind to damn me for not being thirty years younger. And don't your books come to the rescue now? Isn't it enough for you to read a novel to make that which you would prefer be there on the other side of your window? That can be done only with the ones I send to hell for lying. In those novels, the murderer is always caught and age doesn't matter as long as there is will; in those, the characters act out of conviction even though the writer does it for money. That is why the lawyer defends the black man without being cowed by the protests of the whites, why the unjustly convicted prisoner digs a tunnel to freedom, why General Miller is kind to his prisoners even though they do not speak his language. In those novels, the tubercular is cured and the alcoholic redeemed, and the writer receives prizes as undeserved as all prizes. Lucio watches the woman at the tree, the water beginning to run down her hair. On the other hand, the books I preserve are life, and life establishes a wall between that woman and me. Laffitte loved Babette, but had to let her be lost behind the door. He knew that literature condemns: blacks are thrown off bridges, children buried, old men tortured, towns die without a drop of water, the beloved woman goes off to Kaliningrad. That is the reality, although now the ground is wet and I am weak and want that woman to stay. What about my mother? asks Remigio. Lucio casts his eyes down; he is satisfied in the knowledge that at least in his memory, Herlinda will never be old. The books are now many, he says, and I haven't even gotten near her. There are city women, sophisticated or aggressive or whores, nothing like Herlinda. And writers who talk about country women and make them out as superstitious, witches, women able to get from one place to another without having to take a step, who go through walls and heal with herbs; none make plans to set up a balanced-feed store-room, none add more salt than necessary to the vegetable soup. Herlinda is difficult to find; a country girl but one with smooth skin; a country girl but one who doesn't believe in the dead coming back to life, or in children wise as old men or who have yellow eyes or the talons of a hawk; a girl from the country and the desert but without healing powers or stupid traits that make readers compare her with their servant girls. I have detected some of her qualities in Russian novels, but over there the women end up crying too much and are ready to prostitute themselves rather than see their father starve to death. Is that why you keep reading? Lucio does not answer and they go out to the orchard. The rain keeps coming down harder; the woman stays in front of the tree. Remigio throws a stone down the well. Did you hear it? If that sound hadn't stopped rising, this woman would be very far away, in Monterrey, indulging her little girl. Of course, Lucio slaps him on the back, looks up at the sky, getting raindrops in his eyes. And you? What would you be doing? Pulling apart henequen fibers to earn a few pesos, weeding your orchard, preparing to plant chili peppers for next season? Look at what that girl brought you. You now live for your tree, waiting for Babette's avocados to come out and love them above all else, not like the ones you smeared on your sheets, which are scarcely better than any woman from around here. They are talking confidently, without lowering their voices, in the assurance that the rain shields them from the woman's ears. Did you touch Babette? Run your hands over her skin? I couldn't avoid it; you told me to check the label on her panties. No need to apologize. Lucio shuts his eyes. That's what she came for, to live forever in you. The rain is the only element out of place. A town like Icamole, with women of the ilk of Señora Urdaneta, deserves to die in the aridness, to end its history with Father Pascual's urine. They should all have left; you alone would remain, hugging your tree, treasuring your avocados, eventually to die at peace between smeared sheets.

But it is raining, Remigio says, and Lucio nods. God has little artistic sense; he spoiled a good ending. He preferred Fatso Antúnez rolling in the street to being thrown off a cliff. Besides, he gave Melquisedec more than enough life. They should have thrown him out of the pickup truck as soon as they made him confess to the crime. However, that should really not be put off; by tomorrow, at the latest, we will hear that he is dead.

It suddenly stops raining, and they both remain silent as the clouds. Lucio goes to the woman, stopping behind her. You don't have to love me, he says; that you serve me is sufficient. And judging from the woman's face when she turns around, it is evident that she has not read *Yoshikazu's Paradise*.

Don Porfirio chased a fly off his food and remembered, without having willed it . . . What was he eating? the woman asked. I don't know, Lucio replied. What is there in Paris for a Mexican to eat? She thought for a moment before suggesting anything. Would a *cocotte de porc à l'ananas* appeal to you? No, it wouldn't. Let us say he was eating boiled chicken, because I imagine that his teeth wouldn't be up to any other kind of meat. But it is not essential to clarify that point. I'm interested in saying something else. So take another approach, says the woman, because I am interested in knowing where the fly lit. Lucio thinks there is nothing like reading and making a judgment: does it go on a bookshelf or to hell? To imagine on the basis of a text is easy, but to imagine on the basis of a blank mind gets complicated. Don Porfirio shooed a fly from the back of his hand and, without willing it, recalled the infestation of flies in Icamole, the swarms of them buzzing around his fallen soldiers. I could have been one of them. A bullet that passes half a meter away from my body represents a minute diversion of the rifle from which it was shot a hundred meters away; it is an imperceptible movement caused by the beating of the heart, which expands the fingertips; it is, for all practical purposes, mere chance. In a battle like that of Icamole, with targets and shooters in movement, everything is a matter of chance, every bullet becomes a shot in the dark. If fortune had elected to drill my skull, my breast in that place, what would have happened to my country, to its history, its people, its monuments? There would have been no Porfiriate, or, of course, a Don Porfirio; instead of having a resolute president for over thirty years, Mexico would have continued in its tradition of one brawl after another, presidencies of a few months, a few days, a few hours, simply in wait for the next uprising, weakening itself and sending signals to other countries: Look at us, we are a bunch of savages with no idea of how to govern ourselves; we need another foreign invasion, another Bourbon prince, another gringo shit to carve another slice out of us. A sudden sneeze at the wrong moment by the rifleman and I would be buried somewhere in the desert known as Icamole, which now might very well be part of the United States. Don Porfirio would never have existed, and the Mexicans would be mourning the savior who never appeared. That is the reason why Icamole should put up a plaque that says, Here Don Porfirio was saved; here our nation was saved.

The woman raises her hand to halt the flood of words from Lucio. Did you know that at the age of fifty-one Don Porfirio married a fifteen-year-old girl? You are over sixty now, and I am no longer fifteen, but maybe the difference in their ages is equivalent to that in ours. I assumed you would be thinking about that, about this, she says, as she slides her hands over her arms, her face, her calves, but I see that your eyes are fixed on your town. I ask for a passage in Don Porfirio's life, and you give me praise for your country; a speech worthy of the cockroaches. You are an imposter, you do not come up to even the level of the soles of Pierre Laffitte's feet. Lucio bows his head. The woman is right. That's how an editor should deal with an author. Andrade Berenguer should have gotten such a scolding, such an insult from his editor, his manuscript flung in his face. When are you going to reveal to me the truth about lovers? Or Felipe Ibarrola himself? Could it be that nobody told him, I don't care that your book can be read forward and backward when it is the same bore coming and going? The woman goes over to Lucio; her voice is not that of an irritated editor but of an understanding woman. I would have preferred you to speak of the first contact between those two nude bodies. What they said to each other. Or was it all in silence? Was that dictator capable, in intimacy, of uttering words of love? Did Carmelita feel desire, or was she thinking that her father had delivered her into sacrifice? Pierre Laffitte would have known that, no matter how many battles he had fought, no matter how pressing the nation's problems, for Don Porfirio at that moment, there was no more Mexico than the virgin flesh in his bed. Of course, says Lucio, but Laffitte has confidence in the mind of the reader; that is why the door closes upon Babette, why the door of Don Porfirio's bedroom will close, leaving us outside to find a peephole in the curtain, the keyhole in the lock, to make us press an ear to the wall, because he distinguishes the moments at which imagination outshines actuality, desire is more intense than pleasure, and doubt, more irksome than proof. Laffitte is eloquent silence. Many readers will yell, Open the door, Don Porfirio, I want to know what you are doing with that girl, want to see her thighs writhing in resistance, how you turn her around to pin her down; or, I want to see her hungry, craving skin and power. The editor will pound harder on that door, will want to kick it in: Open up immediately or we will lose a lot of readers; open up or nobody will be interested in making a film of this story. But Don Porfirio will not open because Laffitte prevents him, and readers will drop away, a few at a time to begin with, then in hordes, to other stories of open doors, with no secrets, in which sooner or later it is known what they did in the bedroom, whose weapon it was, why she refused to marry, who killed her, how they did it, what ingredients are in the grandmother's cookies, who was the actual father, what became of the girl's shoe. Lucio keeps quiet because he can tell by the woman's eyes, her forced smile, that she is not an ally, and he elects to change the subject. Shortly after I opened the library, I named it the Klaus Haslinger, after which the government demanded that I baptize it with the name of a teacher with no other attribute than that of being a higher-up in the Teachers' Union. Now I am independent and can name it whatever I please, that is, if you authorize me to use you daughter's name. Anamari? the woman asks. Do you like that, the Anamari Library? Lucio goes over to her and moves a curl off her forehead. The woman is not annoyed and does not draw her head away. He wishes gravity would return the curl to where it had been so that his fingers might pick it up again and put it back, for curls to be falling everywhere over her face and body. Anamari is a nice name for a girl, but on the front of a building it might be appropriate for a luncheonette; I was considering Babette.

The clouds have not yet passed, giving the surroundings an aspect of the lateness of late afternoon, despite its being the middle of the day. Lucio comes out of the place cursing the new barrage of rain. Surreptitiously, he looks at the other end of the street to see if by chance his shoe might be poking out in the orography of stones, dead branches, and puddles. He is ashamed of the worn-out pair he is wearing and of the thought of the woman seeing him that way, ragged as a peasant who has recently arrived in the city in a Scandinavian novel. Have you read *Our Daily Bread*? he asks, and when the woman nods, Lucio points at his shoes. Of course, she says, Oleg is certain that if his toes were not so crooked it would be more dignified for him to go barefoot. Oleg is out of work, hungry, with nowhere to lay his head at night; he is huge, a rough, powerful man who dug ditches and carried rocks in the country. But standards in the city are different; Oleg's arms are of no use if he doesn't know how to add, and we are moved by his defenselessness when he offers his services to remove the garbage at a restaurant because we know that he will not be throwing it away. Lucio finds an iron bar, which he jams under the sign bearing the name of the teacher Fidencio Arriaga. One heave is enough to wrench it off the wall. Oleg sinks to the depths of degradation, and, when winter comes and we believe he will freeze to death in an alley, the owner of the bakery offers him bread and hot tea. I need a worker like you, she tells him, a man like you. The author does not dare starve him to death or freeze him in a blizzard, she says, although that would have been the logical ending. Lucio picks up the sign and throws it in the street. He is surprised at how well the letters of Klaus Haslinger's name have survived below the sign. He received the Pavlov Prize thanks to that book, she says. If Oleg had died, good-bye Pavlov. Oleg proves that, despite his shoes, there is some-body who can give him a new lease on life. That happens because the author is male, she asserts; he portrays a good soul and believes that a woman could love him for that reason alone. He is mistaken: we women need other information about such a man. We know nothing of the warmth of his voice, whether he looks into your eyes when he talks, if his embrace gives us a feeling of littleness. A woman is not interested in a man who needs to be saved. As an employee, perhaps, she concludes, but for loving a man, the good soul part is the least of it.

Looking through the window of her bakery, Greta noticed that the snow was falling more heavily every minute. The streets were beginning to empty and, assuming that there would be no more customers that afternoon, she decided to close up and go home. On the way, she paid no attention to a mound at one side of the path, and throughout the winter she wondered why Oleg of the dark, sunken eyes never came by her shop again hoping she would offer him a stale bread left over from the day before yesterday.

Do you prefer it that way? Much better, she says. Oleg dead under the snow is preferable to the original novel, preferable also to your failed history of Don Porfirio. You obviously know better how to handle a poor devil than a president.

The goat is tethered to the tree. Remigio approaches the animal and clasps him tightly between his legs. With his left hand he grips him by the hair and hide at the nape of the neck and raises the knife toward him with his right hand. The animal moves his legs in a feeble effort to get free, a futile effort, merely to make a show of unwillingness. He looks at the purple plastic basin waiting to catch the blood.

Wait, says Lucio, don't kill him the usual way.

Hours earlier, Lucio had knocked on various doors asking if the time had come for any goat to be put down. Señor Treviño was the one who said, Yes, I have a stud that's lost interest. Lucio offered to take the animal off his hands. I'll have him back for you tomorrow cleaned, ready to eat or sell, assuring the man that there would be no charge, that he just wanted it to teach his son something. Señor Treviño made a dismissive gesture, saying no explanations were necessary, that it was enough for him to get the meat back complete with the innards. You can keep the blood and skin, if you want, but I would like the rest. Remigio separates his legs, releasing the goat, which walks to the other side of the tree. The animal moves slowly, not trying to escape. He begins to nibble on the grass around the tree. Your left hand was okay, Lucio says. You will take him by the nape of the neck, but you are going to change other things. The knife, for instance, is not for cutting his throat; you are going to plunge it into the belly, just under the sternum. You are going to be in front of him; you are going to lift him up so that he is on two legs and you can look straight into his eyes. Remigio twists his mouth to one side, considers for a moment, nods, goes into his house and returns quickly, barefooted and in his underwear shorts. Lucio snorts. At what point did my son get so finicky? I try to get something important across to him and he worries about his clothes being stained.

All set, says Remigio, as he grabs the goat by the neck and gets it up on its hind legs. Just point out to me which is the sternum. The animal keeps chewing on a blade of grass. Lucio puts his forefinger where the soft part of the abdomen starts. Here, he says, you stab all at once or little by little, as you like. Remigio places the knife point in the exact spot. He does not plunge it in until he is looking straight into the yellow eyes with the sausagey pupil, and then he thrusts hard. At first the only apparent difference it makes is that the goat stops chewing; there is no bleating. Instead, yes, a hissing from the throat, a rapid expansion and contraction of the nostrils. Give the knife a twist, Lucio orders; the animal must be aware that it is you injuring him. Remigio does not see the wound because he is looking directly into his victim's eyes. But he does not have to see it; he feels the blood running down his fist, feels the hooves on his arm kicking weakly, hears the spurt of urine spatter the ground. He twists the knife a little more and the goat's eyelids go half-shut, the face as a whole takes on an expression that Remigio is unable to fathom but that intrigues him. The goat has just closed his eyes, although there is still life in him. Do I keep on? It doesn't matter, Lucio answers, surely you already saw what you had to. Remigio withdraws the knife and lets go of the animal, which balances himself trembling on unsteady legs, the blade of grass sticking out of his mouth.

Let's see if you are smarter than Santín and his colleagues. Did you witness horror and the eyes like saucers? No, nothing like that. And do you know why the goat is the ideal animal for sacrificing? With no answer forthcoming from Remigio, Lucio replies, Because it dies like a man, though with more dignity, because the goat is not worrying about plans for the future, unfinished projects, or about his mother, his children, a woman by the name of Evangelina. That is why he is docile, and if he kicks, it is a reflex; he isn't trying to hurt you. Priests don't speak of a scapechicken, because it will run around with its head cut off; or of dogs because they snap. Sure, man tries to defend himself, is horrified and all that writers say, but before the end he becomes just like a goat and doesn't feel terror but something else, did you notice? Remigio tries to figure out the goat's expression, turns to watch the trembling animal, which, in an act of docility, has walked over to the basin and stood there so that his blood will run into it. Shame, he says, it seems to me he feels ashamed. Lucio beams. Exactly. I did not expect a man standing in his underwear to come up with the answer, but now I see that your vision goes deeper than Santín's and his friends'. And I can assure you that a dying woman with a bullet in her breast, certain that this is the end of her, will feel ashamed just as if she were caught nude in the public square or was being spied on in the bathroom, and, if given time, will worry about the dress she is going to be buried in. There's nothing like that in novels about murder, only violence, blood, and, especially, horror with all its synonyms, which are many; sometimes there is anger, insults, or tears, but never shame. Señora Urdaneta is bitten by a snake while having a squat out in the fields. How will she apply the little strength she has left? Don't know, Remigio responds, straighten her skirt that got bunched up around her waist, maybe. Correct, says Lucio, but first she would wipe herself if she has paper; it is not a question of trying to survive but of dying under conditions of decency. Santín however would set her to shrieking I don't want to die, providing eyes filled with terror, and pour in stuff with which to shape a fake death. The goat will quickly get the idea that it is the end and bend its head down. What about Pedro Montes? Remigio asks. Also, says Lucio, he was stretched out there for several days, which is why he wrote the letter, but I assure you that he was ashamed during the final moments, especially about smelling of urine.

Remigio shrugs. Maybe what you say is true, but if the readers can't differentiate between a real death and a make-believe one, it doesn't matter whether the writer does or not; that's why they applaud Santín. And, anyway, novels are only words, and the word *death* is not the same as death.

Lucio thinks of Herlinda, of how he found her in bed, with the sheet pulled modestly up to her chin, when undoubtedly there was a moment at which she realized that the pain in her legs was not just fatigue but something serious, and even so decided to stay in bed rather than go out in the street to get help; better to die quietly, discreetly, than to be exposing to the eyes of all Icamole her swollen legs beginning to turn purple. Go tell Lucio that Herlinda is dying, the first woman to find her lying on the ground would say, and Herlinda, knowing that she had only a moment left, would open her soul to that woman, maybe Señora Urdaneta: Please tell Lucio that I love him very much and tell Remigio that I will be looking out for him from the other world. No, if the choice was to speak those words, better to die in silence, as she did, without Señora Urdaneta poised to whisper the posthumous message into my ear as the coffin is lowered into the grave: Incidentally, your wife told me that she loved you very much.

For a moment, Lucio eyes Remigio in his undershorts, his legs spattered with blood. He seems to him a vulnerable figure, despite the stalwart stance, knife in hand. He feels sorry for him and hugs him in a way he has not done since he was a small boy. Incidentally, he says to him, your mother will be looking out for you from the other world.

Beside the avocado tree, the goat drools.

They wait in silence while the white paint is drying under which the name of Klaus Haslinger lies buried. Lucio picks up the teacher Arriaga's sign and fans the wall, because the dampness of the afternoon is delaying the process. Remigio says he will be right back and goes into the library. After *The Apple Tree*, he thinks he might try another novel, goes to the first bookcase, and, indifferent to name of author, title, or commentary, shuts his eyes and reaches for a volume. He likes the cover: the remains of a beached boat; however, it seems too bulky. He puts it back and picks a slimmer one. He turns to the last page to check the length: page 207. Not bad, he says to himself, making a mental calculation: 83 pages less than *The Apple Tree*. It's about dry now, shouts Lucio, time to make the sign. Remigio comes out and puts the novel on the ground next to the paint cans. Pay attention, Lucio says, looking him straight in the eye and speaking slowly, *Biblioteca* is spelled with a B as in *burro*; the same with Babette. *Biblioteca Babette*, four B's and three T's. Sounds good; people will come and read. Don't make any mistakes. Spell it correctly. Better see the cover. I'll get it for you. I want no mistakes when you write *Babette*; don't do like that cop who spelled it with only one T and a V instead of a B. He is in and out in a moment with *The Death of Babette*, leans it against the wall, and says, There are seven letters, even though only five are pronounced. Remigio has barely gotten past the first capital B, fat and black, when they hear a voice behind them. Who is Señor Lucio? They both turn their heads toward a young woman in a white lab coat or nurse's jacket. Out in the street Remigio sees a white car with a shield he does not recognize on the door. Either of you Señor Lucio? Her lips hardly move as she speaks. By that time, both have reached a silent judgment: she is undesirable, primarily because of smallness of eyes and prominent cheekbones, too bulgy in the backside and too flat in the chest. Me, responds Lucio. She introduces herself with no change of expression or extending her hand. I am Licenciada Campos, in charge, and I am here to notify you with great sorrow of the death of Señor Melquisedec Marroquín. You people took your time, says Lucio, and the ceremonious front and deep sorrow are unnecessary. Turning to Remigio, he says, You see, I told you the news would come at the latest today. Dead. Melquisedec is dead, or should I say he was murdered? The *licenciada*'s expression switches to one of puzzlement. May I come in? I have papers for you to sign. Lucio wonders what kind of papers the woman might be carrying. Maybe a statement: We went out for a drive one bright sunny morning, Melquisedec was in the back of the pickup truck. Suddenly, I saw in the mirror he wasn't there, he'd fallen out, an unfortunate accident. No, Licenciada, he says, I have nothing to do with that man's death and have never driven pickup trucks. It is about another matter, she says. Could we go in? Remigio watches them go into the library and pricks up his ears while painting the other fat capital B below the first one. Lucio settles down behind his desk and makes a sign to the *licenciada* to have a seat. She opens her briefcase and takes out a folder. We must act fast, she says. The body is still in the *rurales'* station and they have no refrigeration. Fast for what? Lucio wants to know, but no answer is necessary: the papers explain everything. After reading halfway through the first page, he looks up at the *licenciada*. I am not related to that man, he says while keeping his forefinger on the line where his name appears in blue ink: Lucio Mireles, brother-in-law, domicile known, Icamole, occupation, librarian. Brother-in-law? Melquisedec was never known to have a wife or my wife to have a sister. He gets to his feet and waves the papers. Occupation, librarian? Seeing those two words in a document bearing the state seal irritates him. Books are no longer my occupation; you people took that away from me; the same seal appeared on the letter of We regret to advise you that as of the month of February of the current year, the Fidencio Arriaga Library will be discontinued, for which reason we request that you appear to pick up your severance pay and a lock that you must affix to the door. Señor, says the *licenciada* patiently, I did not come to discuss your life. I was sent to find somebody to take charge of the body of Señor Marroquín, and it seemed to us that you were the person indicated because the deceased named you as his closest relative. The woman shuffles the papers until she comes to the line she wants. Besides, she says, in the file of the case, the police declare that Melquisedec Marroquín was arrested because the librarian of the place identified him as the suspected party responsible for the girl's disappearance and likewise suggested that the accused could be guilty of other kidnappings of children, whom he would hide in the drums he used for carrying water. The latter, however, was not investigated, since no report other than that of this girl has been received. Now do you understand? The *licenciada* drops the papers on his desk. In a way you are responsible for Señor Marroquín's fate. From the sarcastic tone of those words, Lucio concludes that the *licenciada* does not believe Melquisedec is guilty. A short story by Michael William Brown comes his mind. During a visit to the zoo, the protagonist pushes a schoolmate into the pit around the enclosure of the Bengal tigers. They can accuse me of a push, he was to say later, but I didn't eat Billy.

Do you know Paolo Lucarelli? Lucio goes to the shelf to fetch *City without Children*. You should know it. That would preclude insinuations as to my responsibility for Melquisedec's fate. An Italian drayman sealed his own fate when he killed Benedetta, the Spadas' daughter; he got away with it that time, but now it was the very voice of Lucarelli that returned to denounce him: It was he, he stuffs girls into his water drums, don't let him get away, don't let our streets and squares be emptied of children. Their eyes meet, unblinking, for a few seconds, until Lucio lowers his to the documents that deal with burial rights, availability of the body for delivery between 8:00 A.M. and 3:00 P.M., including Saturdays and Sundays, on presentation of ID with photograph, as well as personal particulars of the deceased; a statement follows signed by Melquisedec himself and the official certificate of the attending physician in which one item has been left blank: cause of death. This is worse than an Ángela Molina novel. Lucio crumples the documents, goes to the door of hell, and tosses them through the opening. The *licenciada* protests with a groan and words that do not emerge. Why is the cause of death not indicated? What are they hiding? She looks into the adjoining room; the light is poor, but she is able to make out the book dump. It's an exemption, she explains. Exemption for whom? For policemen who throw old men out of pickup trucks? Nobody threw anybody out of anywhere, the *licenciada* says; the man slit his wrists, and the exemption protects him, you, the relatives; that way, the church doesn't find out and a priest can say Mass for him. Go away, Lucio turns his back on the *licenciada*, get out of here. I don't know the man. He never came to read a book, and I barely took a drink or two of water from his drums. I don't care if he bled to death in a cell or on the side of the highway or if they are waiting for my signature to slip a knife under his sternum. Give me back my papers, the *licenciada* says in a tone that achieves little force of authority. Get out. She leaves slowly, goes to her car, and is soon out of sight.

Lucio comes out to supervise the sign making. It seems to be going well. If Remigio makes no mistakes, he will ask him to fill in the missing letters on the *Bibliote* sign over the door. What is it that you are going to read? He tries to speak calmly, but his hands still tremble with rage. Remigio paints one more letter. He knows that no answer is necessary: the book is on the ground, and Lucio is only making conversation. *Pater Noster?* He picks it up. Don't read this; it's one of those books that everybody praises but few understand. I'll give you another, something more accessible for the beginner.

Remigio did not enjoy reading *The Apple Tree*, the time in bed, under the light of a lamp, looking at blocks of print that didn't move forward in step with the images. Right now he was able to hand down a decision on the *licenciada*'s homeliness in no time; Santín, on the other hand, would have needed a good couple of pages to describe her and even then wouldn't have done justice to the sallowness of her skin, the wart on her neck, the thickness of her ankles, or the heave of her hips with every step. While listening to her interview with Lucio in the library, the tone of voice of each let one know who was speaking, with no need to specify Lucio said, the *licenciada* said, this one asked, the other replied, exclaimed, explained, declared, clarified. Besides, reading in bed forced him into a position that began to hurt his neck, and the weight of the book tired his arms, which wasn't conducive to the floaty sleep he could have enjoyed among avocados at that time of night. And on finishing the book what did he have? A story about a murder, a burial, and a tree that grew apples with a boy's face on them; a bunch of nonsense of no use to him even for making conversation with drunks. However, his father told him in a discussion the night before that Santín understood very little, didn't know life and, much less, death or what happens when burying somebody under a tree, and for Remigio that made him feel special; now he could give his opinion of a person he didn't know, rich and famous for sure, a writer after all, respected and admired, and his autograph requested by people, while he, a small-town boy without fame or fortune, calls him an idiot because, besides, imagination should have a limit, and who could think up writing about apples with eyes, nose, and a mouth. When he got to the last page he cursed Santín out and slammed the book shut, but the sensation was different from that of swearing at a soccer player or politician. Now he can go to Villa de García of a Sunday, sit down in a cantina to watch soccer, and wait for a bad play so that, while everybody is insulting the player, he is able to say, For me, that Santín is more of a jerk, and take another slug of beer, satisfied with himself because nobody will know what he is talking about.

Lucio places *Tuberculosis* on top of *Pater Noster*. It's better, he says; children and adults are dying while a doctor wonders whether to help the patients or return to his sweetheart.

The second T in Babette came out a little fatter and lopsided than the first. Yes, I will accept Melquisedec's body, says Remigio; I'm going for it tomorrow. Are you crazy? says Lucio giving the teacher Arriaga's sign a kick. Let those murderers take care of burying it. It's the least I can do, Remigio replies, for the old man, for his mother, for that Sunday in the park and the wooden pony. Lucio mumbles an insult and goes up to his room, stamping hard on each step. Remigio takes pains with the final letter in Babette, mute as the girl under the tree, still as stones.

Melquisedec's mules have been loose these days. Remigio coaxes them with grass from his orchard and hitches them to the wagon, the empty drums still loaded. He supposes that with nobody to take responsibility for looking after them they would have died had it not rained. He checks the harness, climbs onto the driver's seat, and kicks gently at the animals' rumps to start them on the trip to Villa de García. The clatter draws some people to their windows; they think Melquisedec is back.

The next day, Remigio tells what happened. They just had him laid out on the floor with a sheet over him in a cell, locked, so's he shouldn't escape on them; only his arms with the slashes on the wrists where the blood ran out showing from under the sheet. They handed me a pile of papers, and I was signing without reading them, but one thing, yes: I explained to them that we were not related; the thing is that our families were always very close; Melquisedec's ended with Melquisedec, and that the only ones left on our side were my father and me, although there was a time when we went to the park together. Never mind that I never mentioned you, but they knew right off from my name and they said, You're the son of the librarian who accused the deceased. And I said that yes I was the son but I didn't know anything about accusations and that, in any case, it didn't matter who was first to point the finger, but who forced him to confess what he did to the girl in all the details. They didn't want me to keep on that track and just checked off a couple of other lines where they needed my signature. Without intending to, I thought of Santín: I guess that's the way he spends his time, signing autographs. Have you read *Tuberculosis* yet? No, I've had no time. Remigio goes into the kitchen. Some time ago, I put aside a couple of beers for a special occasion; I suppose this is a good time to break them out. He opens them, unchilled, and hands one to his father. They told me I'd come for Melquisedec's body just in time. Some medical students want it, one of the cops who arrested him said; they agreed that if nobody was there to pick it up by three o'clock today, it was theirs. I looked at the clock; it was a quarter to three. I didn't believe them. The last thing they would do is turn that body over to people who would be opening it to check out diseases or to find out if he had stones in his liver. Right off they would have recognized it for a tortured body and that maybe the cutting of the wrists was after death. Lucio smiles and clinks his bottle with Remigio's. Cheers, he says. After all, maybe they did throw him out of the pickup truck. I got rid of the drums on the way to Villa de García; I had to have space to stretch out the body. I untied them and threw them down a slope somewhere so's they wouldn't be obstructing the highway. That was when it occurred to me that if the cops had even a suspicion that Melquisedec killed the girl they would have impounded the drums. I checked inside them, but there was no sign of Babette's shoe. When we finished the paperwork, I asked them to help me get the body up on the wagon. It's not all that simple, the other cop said to me with that nice-guy tone that signals a screwing is imminent. We can't let just anybody go through the streets with a dead person like he was bringing dirty laundry down to the river. From the outset, I suspected that those *rurales* were up to something, because they never once took off their hats. We have to obey the laws and procedures, the cop said, then put a hand on my shoulder and showed me a card. What you have to do now is call this number and hire an undertaker. I knew that this was not the moment to be letting them in on my plans; my idea was to take the body wrapped in the sheet and drop it in a grave at the potter's field where they bury the bodies from the Battle of Icamole; forget caskets and funeral rites with priests. Having to compare the gorgeous body I found on my property with the ugly bulk of Melquisedec was an adventure for me; I also wanted to confirm whether there was any connection between that dead man and the goat. Morbid, said Lucio, that's the word for it; you had no call to be confirming anything. There was something more. Remigio opts for directness and gets the envelope of photographs out of his wardrobe. See this boy? Lucio brings the image up close to his eyes and studies it for a moment. I never saw so sorrowful a face as that on anyone sitting on a pony, he says; he looks like a Czech novelist. It's Melquisedec. Remigio touches the face on the film, Wouldn't it have been better for him to have died that same day in the park? He could have stuffed himself on cotton candy or blown up the balloon seller's gas tank. I want to connect the boy in the photograph with the body I saw laid out in the cell, and I say lucky Babette, because she never had to go through deterioration. Compare an old horse with a colt, an old goat with a kid; make the same comparison with any animal and you will see that no body degenerates the way man's does. Lucio looks at his hands and elects to avoid the subject. So, did they turn it over to you? he asks. I told them I had no money for a funeral parlor, and so one of the *rurales* had two boys come right in. These are the students I was talking about, he said. They are willing to take the body away without charging. Okay, I said, but then let's cancel the papers. The boys lifted Melquisedec and threw him on a stretcher with wheels; the sheet slipped off, and I saw the abused body covered with bruises. They had him practically naked and, just as I had figured, his undershorts were green. The sheet was whisked back over him before I knew it, all so fast that I don't know whether the Melquisedec I have in my mind is a memory or a fantasy, but you are right, even his dead face looked ashamed, more than anything, ashamed, because, no doubt about it, in any case, whatever way they murdered him, his throat wasn't cut with a knife nor was his blood collected in a purple basin. He died in a way he oughtn't to have, without even chewing a blade of grass, and under conditions he would have gladly traded for a knife under the sternum. At that moment I was glad to leave him to the students; I always knew there would be differences between Babette and the old man, but I didn't expect so many: the shiny legs without any muscle; pleated knees; nonexistent backside; neck turned into a half-rotten peach; navel, a black blood clot. I maintain that not a dog, cock, or opossum that dies of old age looks as wasted as an old man. And so, sprawled out on the stretcher hauled by the two boys to who knows where, was without a doubt the way he was imagining his fate on the day of the photograph, and just then his name became apt, fitting him: Melquisedec is who I saw on that stretcher, not the one who lived in Icamole. When they took him away, I asked again to have the papers canceled. The nice cop told me, Don't push it, buddy, because the deceased came up with a confession that he had an accomplice, and the investigation is still not closed; we're missing the little body. I suppose the trap was for you, but it was all the same to them if it was me. They went too far with the torture and needed papers to prove that the corpse delivered to the full satisfaction of a relative or friend of the family was the cadaver of a suicide. Lucio settles back in his chair, satisfied, and runs over the things that have recently been changing. I rediscovered the possibility of talking with my son, and I have a woman visiting me in the library who discusses books. I feel graced by Babette's death, not the novel but the death. You are responsible for two bodies now, he says. Remigio drinks the rest of his beer. He would rather be signing Babette's papers. By this document I hereby declare that I have received to my thorough satisfaction one body of a girl of between twelve and thirteen years of age, of delicious texture, proportions, and size, which I will make sure to touch only one time and desire for the rest of my life. I likewise declare that the said body is that of one who in life went by the name of Babette, and I would like to believe that it was fate, not an old man, that brought her to me in his wagon. I pledge to protect the avocado tree under which she lies against pests and drought and animal urine, to beat Fatso Antúnez black and blue if I catch him jumping the fence to steal one of the fruits; I pledge to multiply its progeny, and, only when its abundance exceeds my appetite, will I proceed to sell off the avocados singly, by the dozen, or by weight, with a sticker attached that says Babette Avocados, Do Not Eat. Lucio also drains his beer. He says that Babette died as much in Paris as in Icamole, that novels also live in the desert even though nobody writes them, because a river is always more useful than dry sand. The Seine is good for having umbrellas thrown into it, the Arno, for carrying children in boxes filled with earth, the Colorado, for having blacks thrown in. What would have become of Russian novels without the possibility of committing suicide in the Neva? Rivers are good for taking a walk along the banks, for floating pleasantly through a city or fighting animals in the jungle, for separating two countries and for drowning Mexicans who try to cross them, and for overflowing. The desert offers nothing but dust, hamlets where nobody drinks wine. That is why in a town without bells Babette had no choice but to appear in the last well that had water. It was your luck, your good luck.

I don't intend to come back to Icamole, the woman says. I'll be leaving Villa de García for Monterrey. I understand, Lucio bows his head, you belong to that other world where the streets have names and people smile like Peter O'Donohue in the *Valley of the Seagulls*. I am alone now, she says, and have more than enough money. I can send you an amount monthly or weekly for you to live on and for the upkeep of the Biblioteca Babette. Lucio folds his arms, advances a few steps toward the woman, then turns his back so that she cannot see his face. The bakery woman saved Oleg; you are saving me. Thank you, but my life is not one for a Pavlov Prize, to enable somebody to say Lucio puts forward the grandeur of the individual vis-à-vis the arbitrariness of history, nature, or fate. All of this had to end up on the manure pile, had to die under the sun. The rain spoiled it. Everybody should have cleared out, one by one or in a body, leaving me holed up alone in my library, reading till my strength gave out; I would then reach for the last book, *Fishes of the Land*, and in Chapter 18, when Fritz and Petra decide to leave, my body would finally be failing. I would die with the book upon my chest, and millions of years later an archaeologist would find me imbedded in stone together with trilobites. A fish of the land, that scientist of the future would say. And observing me under a microscope, tapping on me with a chisel, he would try to explain my life:

carnivorous, walked on four feet, mated once a year and laid eggs; he was a reader, the last of his species; a temperature change killed him; his penis was small. Pure nonsense, book-flap commentary. Oleg should have ended up as a pile of snow undiscovered until springtime. That would have lent him grandeur. He would have had to spurn Greta's bread because in saving himself he falsified his very life. A man should end up under a pile of snow or earth, bleeding to death in a cell, thrown out of a pickup truck or off a bridge, in a well or septic tank, or entangled in the roots of a tree; the rains ought not come, or the bakery woman have reason to offer him bread; nor should a wooden pony make the difference between tears and a smile. That is the only worthy ending for a novel or a life, even though there be no praise or Pavlov Prizes. And instead of your offering me money, you would do well to accept the end as Babette accepted it, as Melquisedec ended up doing. You oughtn't even lie to me by saying you are going to Monterrey; I know you are going much farther, to Kaliningrad, and I do not even have a box done up in brown paper to throw to you. Father Pascual did understand proper endings, which is why he ordered that they abandon the town and, on remaining alone, pissed on the dry ground to watch the way it was absorbed, leaving no trace of his once having been there. But what could the ending of Icamole be if it had already been ruined by the rain? The woman thinks Lucio has asked her a question and she feels obliged to say something. Your library could catch fire and you die inside, or the cockroaches knock down the door and eat you up and you scream but nobody dares rescue you. Precisely, says Lucio, artistry is lost and, now, we are left only with noisy, cheap movie endings.

His back still to the woman, he opens his fly and pisses; however, the earth, now saturated with moisture, causes the urine to collect in one small hollow. There's no point, he says. There has to be a different ending.

You were not satisfied with poor Babette, poor thing, bells and more bells, a country that believes it is free, a girl who has no beliefs. You liked *The Death of Babette* on paper but not in life; that's why you asked Laffitte for a different ending and wound up mixing it with *The Apple Tree*, an inferior work. The woman bends down to pick up a stone that contains a fossil of ancient life and puts it in her pocket. I'd better be on my way, she says, and starts down the hill. At the bottom, Melquisedec's mules are grazing. Two boys have cleaned her windshield and stand by waiting for a tip. Lucio watches her drawing slowly away, treading insecurely on the uneven paving stones. I have read countless similar scenes and, generally, the woman turns around to say something, the expected or unexpected twist that transforms sad endings into happy ones. By the way, Amanda came to see me yesterday, assured me that she still loves you; by the way, the money is safe in a locker at the airport; by the way, Uncle Ray changed his will before he died; by the way, I have more than enough room in case you care to come live with me; by the way, the doctors were able to save Herlinda, she will be coming home on Monday.

The woman hands the boys some coins, and the car rolls off considerately, raising no dust cloud. Lucio starts down the hill to his library.

He has no problem with Remigio's ending. Remigio closes himself in his room to read *Tuberculosis*. He gets halfway through Chapter 7, in which a young couple is holding hands without speaking. The young man is unable to speak because of a sudden fit of coughing, she, because of being in the middle of a treatment: Doctor Mendrok is replenishing the air lost as a result of her pneumothorax. This word makes Remigio give up reading. A term of that kind can only mean that the girl is sure to die within a few pages. And, despite the hopelessness of his work, Doctor Mendrok has notified his wife that he does not intend to return to Vienna, that his place is in the clinic. He does not realize that his effort to save lives scarcely suffices for prolonging the existence of the condemned ones, who necessarily end up loving one another, and so what was previously resignation evolves with time into tragedy. He closes the book and keeps turning from his left, where he has placed the photograph of Melquisedec the boy, to the window on his right, through which he is able to see the tree of novice avocados. He longs for the day when all the little Babettes or Anamaris ripen and are ready and appropriate for merging with his desert man's rough skin. Here we are, do you remember our smooth skin, the gray eye that doesn't close, and the panty label? Here we are, a silhouette drawn upon your sheet with avocados. Here we are, we love you, I love you, call me Babette, call me Anamari; we will be one smeared flesh. Do with us what you will; all we ask of you is that you never again allow us to be thrown into the well. It is very deep, very dark, and if we don't die from the impact, we will die of fright. No, says Remigio, I will never allow anyone to touch you but me. Come, my Babettes, my Anamaris, my full-time and part-time little whores, my eternal women whom morning finds inevitably smashed and lifeless. But not even in those ecstatic moments will Remigio be able to smile, not anymore, never anymore, because Melquisedec is looking at him from the wooden pony, and Melquisedec is not giving permission.

Lucio closes and locks his library door. Now what happens? He sits down at the desk and lets his head droop onto his folded arms. There are matches in the drawer, paper catches fire immediately, obliterates everything. Fires are a good option for ending a story that doesn't seem to be coming to a close. Stables burn down with the horses inside, why not a library set on fire to put an end to me? An element of chance is introduced, an oversight, a kerosene lamp on the hay in the stable; the farmer goes in to save his horse and perishes in the flames. Or I could strip naked and cross that doorway into hell; I am a shoddy novel, a son of Santín. Thousands of roaches swarming over the bloodless body not caring any longer. Let those creatures have their way are his last words, and he lets them bite, enter every cavity of his body; he spills his bodily fluids over books by Ángela Molina and Ricardo Andrade Berenguer. He shakes his head and curses the rain, curses the god seduced by Pavlov.

Somebody is knocking at the door, but Lucio does not move; impossible for it to be a reader arriving at this hour: Señora Urdaneta asking for a romantic novel she is interested in, Fatso Antúnez with sensitivity despite his idiocy, one of the cops disposed to comb through the pages of *City without Children*. The knocking continues briefly. He refuses to open. It is unacceptable to him that on top of urine the ground refused to absorb they should now be sending him a reader; that instead of fire the library inspector has come to tell him that he can now count on reinstatement of his salary. Go away, he says in a whisper, and lies down on the floor waiting for the phantom to leave his door. He hears a final series of knocks, tentative now, lacking conviction, and then slow footsteps fading away. After waiting a moment he hurries to the window. The street appears deserted. He returns to his desk, unbuttons his shirt, presses the WITHDRAWN stamp to his chest, and slumps to the floor. He has not read *The Blue Snows*, he says to himself, and perhaps won't; not knowing the contents of the little brown box no longer worries him, for he will never be giving it to the woman who went off to Kaliningrad. Staring at the stains on the ceiling, he turns into a black man talking about equality, an apple with the face of a boy, a cigarette being desultorily puffed against a jazz background; he is a translator's note, a French entrée, O'Donohue smiling; he is the impossibility of revealing the truth about lovers. He inserts a finger under his sternum and pushes hard, pulling it away as soon as it hurts. He didn't have the guts of Zimbrowski's father to accuse his son or, perhaps, to refuse the bakery woman's offer of two-day-old bread. He closes his eyes. He hears shots, galloping horses, the moans of the dying. He shouts to Don Porfirio, asking him not to leave without picking up the wounded, warns him that the soldier Montes lies dying behind a rock. Hours go by. It is beginning to get dark, and there stretched out on the floor he feels as vulnerable as a girl swallowed up in a doorway, weak as a tubercular patient. He mutters a curse for himself and feels like weeping as the Wailer of Icamole wept. Then he understands that nobody knocked on the door. It was the waves. The sea has returned. It will swell until it has staved in the door, flooded his library, exterminated the fish of the land, and washed away every word that issued from a novelist's pen. He would like to have had a chance to say good-bye to Babette, to his son, most of all to Herlinda, to Herlinda's skin. He knows he won't be able to recognize them when they are trilobites.

He feels shame.

Lucio comes out of his library, aching after such a long time on the floor. The sun is beating down fiercely. It is the hour when women come together to pray a rosary at the Archangel Gabriel chapel. They are only giving thanks now, not asking for anything; Melquisedec is not in their prayers. Lucio approaches them and touches one on the shoulder. Excuse me, he says, but I have to remove this chair. The woman, avoiding discussion, simply moves over to another chair. The peaches-in-syrup jar with the soldier Montes's letter is absent from the altar, perhaps removed for restoration. Lucio hoists Herlinda's chair to his shoulder and leaves; of cast iron, it is quite heavy, the screws holding it together, rusty. I don't know why I was so long in taking it back, Lucio says to himself, the weight causing him to stop and rest a couple of times on the way. When he gets home, he places the chair next to the kitchen table and sits down to have a glass of the state-truck water. He agrees with Remigio: not a comfortable chair. He cannot understand how Herlinda was able to sit in it for so many hours.

There, waiting for him on the checkerboard tablecloth, is the copy of *The Blue Snows*. Lucio knows that Bronislava intended to hold back her tears as the train drew away; maybe she isn't as emotional as other Russian women. Also, the translator explains in a footnote that *galuschki* is a Ukrainian dish. Hopefully, there will be a scene in which Bronislava has put too much salt on the *galuschki* and Radoslav eats it without complaining.

He reads far into the night, paying little attention to the plot and dialogue; he is concerned only with the segments in which Bronislava appears. Although she is a woman to fall in love with, Lucio is disappointed that she should be so concerned about which dress to wear at the reception or about proper French pronunciation. When he comes to the part where the train is leaving for Kaliningrad, Lucio has gleaned no more than one sentence, and it does not refer directly to Bronislava but to one of her servants: Although she worked in the fields, she kept her hands, as well as her skin in general, as smooth as an adolescent's. But that was all, because there was not even anything useful regarding the Ukrainian dish, which is mentioned only once in the course of a dialogue in which Radoslav exclaims, I hate my mother's *galuschki*!

He had extracted Herlinda's smooth skin, but so much more of her was still missing.

He decides that it is time to find her and that he will have to go through the depths of hell to get to his wife. He takes an iron bar and starts to rip away the boards that close off the stairs to the withdrawn-book room. The crashing shatters the silence of the night, the wood gives way and falls upon stairs unused for years. Flashlight in hand, Lucio goes down. Roaches flee from the light, others go unmindfully about their business. He looks at the piles of books and is surprised at how many souls were born to be condemned, souls that should have undergone extermination long before reaching print, souls of those who traded the quill for the cocktail, their personages for their own persona, those who genuflect to a Pavlov, souls of all those sonsofbitches who preach that Latin America has nothing to contribute to letters anymore unless smothered in a gringo sauce, feminine souls that should have been sitting and knitting, lying at their husbands' side, dishing up the day's vegetables instead of assuming that they had been given the word for something other than gossiping with the neighbors. Lucio steps between the piles of books and spits from one side to the other. He shines the beam at his feet to discover that he is standing on *Lost Causes*, one more book by another neophyte government official. He kicks it away and, in passing, curses out every president, ex-president, member of Congress, or ambassador who has tried to pass himself off as a novelist without ever letting go of his wine glass or dirtying his feet in any of the countless Icamoles of this country; he curses any governor who ever signed an order to close a library. You are all in your element here in this hell, he tells them, and I want you to know that I don't need a single peso from your budget to keep Biblioteca Babette open. He continues to walk among the lost souls, stomping with each step. Down with you all, down with you, he growls furiously, because not one of you gave me a sentence that fit Herlinda, because not one said that Herlinda had a scar on her left arm that Lucio liked to stroke, not one said that Herlinda had a silent laugh, blowing air through her nose, not one said anything about Herlinda having almost no eyelashes because of an eye infection when she was fifteen. Herlinda, nobody said Herlinda. Because what heroine is named Herlinda? He is offended at the sight of so many books in that hell, since he now realizes how much time he lost on account of those heaps of garbage-pail pages. He goes to the door and pushes on it until lock and latch give way. He goes straight to the pile of sealed cartons and pulls out one that has been there for six years. He goes back the same way and enters the hell once more. He listens to his steps crunching upon the books, imagining the many roaches that will have perished.

By the time he goes upstairs his feeling of hatred has ebbed.

He puts the carton on the table and clips the bands. There are twenty-two books in it. After making sure that the author is not a gringo, a Spaniard, or a woman, he picks out *The Glass Man*. This time he pays no attention to plot, characters, or dialogue, but only to words, one by one. With scissors he cuts out those with which he can form a sentence. This takes him a couple of hours: Her right eyelid trembled slightly while she slept. *Eyelid* was the word that took him longest to find.

It was daybreak by the time he finished two more: Herlinda fell off the chair on which she was standing to take down a spider web in one corner; and, She preferred to stay in bed that morning. And it isn't that there happened to be a woman named Herlinda in *The Glass Man*, but that he had formed the first syllable of her name by clipping the word *Her*.

She preferred to stay in bed that morning, Lucio read out loud. You are here again, he says, in bed, and now your legs hurt because you fell off the chair, and this time I will let no scorpion in.

He considers that to be enough for this chore and says to himself that he has to have Scotch tape to keep the words from blowing away. He hardly has time to shut the book he had clipped when there is a knock on the door. He hesitates before opening. When he finally he does, he is surprised to see Rebecca at that hour, in a short skirt and vest with shoulder straps. She is not wearing stockings now. Go away, he whispers to her, go back to your life with Doctor Amundaray; you are not welcome here anymore. She embraces him, is reluctant to leave, but he cuts her short with three quick words: Herlinda is back. Rebecca understands, gives him a kiss, and hurries out.

Who was it? Herlinda asks. I don't know; no one was there when I opened the door, but I suppose it was Remigio, he comes at this hour sometimes to ask me for avocados. Would you like for us to pay him a visit? Herlinda is pleased. I haven't seen him in a long time, she says.

They go there side by side, discussing the best way to feed goats, the proper age for mating and slaughtering them. Herlinda looks around and remarks that nothing has changed. Lucio asks her not to be fooled by appearances; he points to Melquisedec's house and tells her that it is vacant. He doesn't dare mention that the feed storeroom was never installed. When they get to Remigio's house, Lucio knocks, and they both wait in silence for at least a minute. Maybe he's asleep, Herlinda says, knock louder. But Lucio shakes his head. Your son has grown up and has a good wife who helps him keep his avocado tree green. Better to come back tomorrow.

They start home. Herlinda, walking slowly, wants to take advantage of the moonlight to recall her Icamole, the surrounding hills, wants to listen to the bleating of the goats, the rushing of the wind. For the first time Lucio welcomes the rain of those days; he would not have liked to be showing Herlinda a dusty town, without greenery, and so their steps on the damp ground are silent, and nobody puts a nose up against a windowpane. He feels his wife's hand, feels its smoothness, and smiles with satisfaction. He tries to frame loving words, but has forgotten how to address Herlinda and does not want to speak to her as though he were addressing Bro-nislava or Rebecca. In the carton that he brought to the kitchen he saw one novel whose cover showed a pair of lovers kissing under an arch of flowers. Lucio thought that it would be a sure candidate for hell, but now supposes that he might borrow a paragraph from it no matter who the author might be; he knows that in bed there is no bad prose.

When they finally reach the front of the house, Herlinda stops short in surprise. A library? I thought you were selling goat feed. I'll explain later, Lucio says, and, embracing and kissing her, begins to fondle her. Many things have happened, Herlinda, and there is still a lot left for us to read.

As soon as they are back in the house, Lucio will nudge her toward the bed to make love to her as he didn't do the last time, putting his hands all over her, memorizing the texture, tracing an indelible map of that body because he urgently needs memories more precious than a salty vegetable soup, than a wife talking about goat feed, than a metal chair with no padding. He is in a hurry because he knows that a scorpion will be back any night to tear his wife from his arms, from the earth, knows that some bad day he might open another carton of books and come up with *Herlinda's Death*, and then there will be no way of avoiding the tragic fate assigned her by its author, whether on the other side of a door or by the act of an old man who steals young wives. Lucio knows that when all is said and done he too has to succumb at any moment, ashamed, with a knife twisted under his sternum; knows that a city writer, an idiot with ideas as puny as his penis, as mediocre as Alberto Santín, must cut him down to nothing in a novel fit for hell and the cockroaches, will bury him in the sands of the sea or the desert every time somebody opens to the last page of *The Last Reader*.